FACING THE SHADOWS

A CHRISTIAN ROMANCE BOOK 2 IN THE SHADOWS SERIES

JULIETTE DUNCAN

COPYRIGHT

PRAISE FOR "FACING THE SHADOWS"

"A very powerful and powerfully written novel with developed and developing characters. Highly recommend" *Robin*

"This author addresses issues which could so easily be used for shock value, but, instead, flawlessly presents with realistic, yet tasteful descriptions and dialogue. This is true Christian based fiction with substance." *Reader*

"I really couldn't stop reading. I picked. It up after getting started. Not knowing that it held my attention to pint that I couldn't put it down. Had to finish it so I could read book#3. Thanks so much for such a dynamic story." *Treach*

"It was a great book. Real life characters. Real life situations that point you to the Lord as your only source of salvation. Clear presentation of the gospel and how to be saved" *Shirley*

ALSO BY JULIETTE DUNCAN

Contemporary Christian Romance
The Shadows Series
Lingering Shadows
Facing the Shadows
Beyond the Shadows
Secrets and Sacrifice
A Highland Christmas (Nov 2017)

The True Love Series
Tender Love
Tested Love
Tormented Love
Triumphant Love
True Love at Christmas
Promises of Love

Precious Love Series
Forever Cherished
Forever Faithful (coming late 207)

Middle Grade Christian Fiction
The Madeleine Richards Series

CHAPTER 1

*L*izzy rapped her fingers on the table, telephone held tightly to her ear. "*Come on Sal, pick up.*" She glanced at the door slammed by Daniel only minutes earlier as he stormed out. Would he come back? And if he did, *what would he do?* Her hands trembled. She had to leave immediately, just in case. But why wasn't Sal picking up?

She threw the telephone back into its cradle, pulled the curtain back, and peered out the window to the street below. At the sight of the Ford Escort fish-tailing down the street into the distance, the reality of what she'd just done hit her like a ton of bricks. A sick feeling flooded her body, and she let out a desperate gut wrenching wail as she fell into the nearby chair and burst into tears.

With her arms wrapped tightly around her stomach, and her body racked by uncontrollable sobs, Lizzy tried to reign in the jumbled thoughts writhing formlessly inside her head.

It hadn't gone to plan. Daniel shouldn't have taken the car, *and where was Sal?* She should have been home. *Now what am I to do?*

A fresh wave of tears assailed her. Sal's mother had taken ill. *How could I have forgotten that?*

She pulled herself slowly up and dried her tears. That left only one option. She'd have to go home, but the very idea filled her with dread.

SHE NEEDED TO GO, or else the temptation of staying might be too great. Standing up, Lizzy straightened her dishevelled clothing and surveyed the apartment with a heavy heart. She picked up the wedding photo sitting on the coffee table and gazed into Daniel's sparkling, mischievous eyes. He'd been so happy and carefree that day. She smiled at the cheeky grin on his face. Then her heart fell. What had happened to them? She hugged her unborn baby and forced back the fresh wave of tears that threatened to besiege her.

Returning the photo to the table, Lizzy sighed dejectedly and walked to the hall cupboard. Her bags were already packed. Deciding what to take had been difficult. Where would she be when the baby was born? By then, hopefully Daniel would have sorted his problems, but three and a half months wasn't a long time, and there was no guarantee. One thing for sure - she wouldn't come back until he had.

Without a car, it was going to be challenging. Lizzy glanced at the clock. If she hurried, there might be time to catch the afternoon train to London. And then... well, she'd think about what to do when she got there.

She picked up the telephone and called a taxi. There was no

way she could bring herself to call her parents just yet. Taking one last look at the apartment, Lizzy wondered if she'd ever be back. Before opening the door, she grabbed the photo and squeezed it into her case.

THE RAILWAY STATION was busier than Lizzy had expected. Taking a train was a new experience. Her family always had a car, and she even remembered when she was little, they also had a driver. These days, Father drove himself.

Maybe going by train would be better anyway. If only she didn't have this heavy suitcase. She thanked the taxi driver as he lifted it out and placed it onto the pavement for her, but then she looked at the stairs.

Inhaling deeply, Lizzy picked up her case, and joined the queue for tickets, her heart rate increasing the closer she got. Could she really do this? Could she really leave Daniel and return to her family home? *Yes.* She had to.

If there was any hope for her marriage, there was no option. Yes, it was a risk, but staying was riskier. Daniel had to sort himself out. She couldn't do it for him. If he loved her as much as he said he did, surely he'd take action and seek help. But would leaving him like she had be enough?

Lizzy moved forward and gulped. It was her turn. The lady behind the counter looked over the top of her glasses with a bored expression on her face as Lizzy hesitated.

"Single to London, thanks. 2nd class." Lizzy's voice wobbled. She handed over the money and took the ticket. When would her heart stop pounding?

Although she'd left most of her belongings behind, her

suitcase was still heavy, and the prospect of carrying it up all those stairs was daunting. But she had to do it. She grabbed it with her right hand, and held the rail with her left. *One step at a time.* She could do this. Where was Daniel when she needed him?

Totally focussed on reaching the top, Lizzy jumped as a hand touched her shoulder. *Daniel? No, it can't be.* She turned around and looked into the eyes of a brown haired young man wearing glasses a little too big for his face.

"Here, let me help you." He reached out and took the case from her hand, warding off her protests. He carried it effortlessly to the top and waited for Lizzy to join him. "What carriage are you in?"

Lizzy took out her ticket and inspected it before answering. "Number three. But I should be alright from here." She smiled at the softly spoken young man who seemed more than eager to help.

"No, no. Let me carry it for you. You shouldn't be carrying it in your condition."

In her condition! She allowed a small grin to show on her face.

"Thank you. That would be lovely." Lizzy babbled about inconsequential things all the way to her carriage. What would he think if she told him she was running away from her husband? It didn't matter. He was only carrying her suitcase.

He helped her onto the train and lifted the suitcase onto the luggage rail above the seats.

"Thank you so much." Lizzy gave the young man an appreciative smile. "There was no way I could have lifted that up there by myself."

"My pleasure. I'm just down the other end of the carriage. I'll come and help when we reach Doncaster."

"There's really no need..."

"It's fine. I don't mind." His sincerity warmed her heart. There really were some nice people in the world.

She smiled at him. "Thank you. That would be wonderful."

He left, and she settled herself into her window seat for the first short leg of her journey.

Alone at last, Lizzy leaned back and breathed in the strange smells. People were still entering, and she hoped no-one would take the seat beside her. The last thing she wanted or needed right now was to engage in idle chatter.

Lizzy's head hurt. Not quite as much as her heart, but a trillion thoughts were running around in her brain, fighting for attention. She took out a notebook and a pen, and started a list. So many things to do, phone calls to make. *Nessa.* She needed to tell her she'd left, and ask her to keep a lookout for Daniel. *The school.* She felt terrible about leaving her class and Kid's Club at such short notice. She'd have to tell the principal it was unlikely she'd be back. He wouldn't be happy about that. She sighed and glanced out the window.

She'd have to call the hospital. Her next checkup was in two weeks. Then she'd have to call her parents. Or maybe she could just turn up unannounced? Was that a coward's way out? Maybe. She'd think about that one. She'd need to pay the rent on the apartment. Daniel didn't have any money as far as she knew. It was either pay it or risk losing all her belongings. She'd have to be careful with her money. The last thing she wanted to do was ask her parents for any.

And where to stay in London? It'd be too late by the time

the train got in to go any further, and besides, a day and night in London on her own held some appeal. Maybe she could stay two nights. No-one knew where she was, after all.

Now that her brain had settled, Lizzy closed her eyes and fell asleep to the clickety clack of the train.

She woke with a start as a loud voice boomed through the speaker. *"Doncaster. Doncaster next station. Change here for Kings Cross London."* She pulled herself up and stretched. How she'd slept in that uncomfortable seat was beyond her.

The train slowed and she gazed out the window as it passed the outskirts of the town. The steeple of the centuries old cathedral was just visible in the distance, but was then blocked by a coal train with seemingly endless carriages.

Once the train had pulled to a stop, she stood and looked up at her suitcase. No, she'd better wait. It'd be stupid to try to get it herself. She smiled at the friendly young man making his way around the other passengers towards her.

"Thank you so much. It's very kind of you." The young man reached up and lifted the case down into the passageway.

"My pleasure. I'll help you onto the next train, but I'm getting off before London. Is someone meeting you at the other end?

Lizzy shook her head. "No, I'm afraid not. I'll manage somehow."

Lizzy followed the young man to the end of the carriage, where he helped her down the step and over the gap between the train and the platform. But how *would* she manage? Her heart began to race as she gazed at the platform that stretched into the distance. And this was only Doncaster.

"The train to London goes from the platform over there. No easy way, I'm sorry. Up the stairs and then back down."

"Why do they make it so hard?" Lizzy grimaced as she looked in the direction he was indicating.

Shrugging, he picked up his own bag before picking up hers, and started walking. "Who knows? I'm Scott, by the way."

"Lizzy. It's nice to meet you, Scott." She smiled warmly at the young man and then walked beside him all the way to the next platform.

The London train was already there and filling up with passengers. Scott helped her into her seat in the seventh carriage, and wished her well. As he walked away, Lizzy was sad she'd never see him again, but content to be left to her own thoughts.

CHAPTER 2

*D*arkness had fallen by the time the train arrived at Kings Cross Station. Lizzy spent the hours reading, thinking, praying and dozing, but now having arrived, being in London on her own caused her stomach to flutter.

The man seated opposite offered to help with her case, and she smiled thankfully at him. She waited for most of the other passengers to alight, and then followed behind. Without Scott to help her, she'd have to take her time.

Even on a Sunday night, London was a noisy, bustling city. Shivering in the cool night air, Lizzy pulled her coat tighter and walked slowly towards the exit, past vendors selling anything from hot dogs to cream buns and ice-creams. The combination of smells assaulted her senses, and she was thankful her morning sickness had passed.

A debate raged in her head most of the way. Should she find a cheap place to stay near the station, or should she go to the fancy hotel her parents always stayed at when they came to

London? She'd be safer at The Kensington for sure, but could she afford it? Lizzy glanced at her watch. Eight o'clock. No, she couldn't risk blowing all her money in one go. She'd find somewhere closer and cheaper.

She made her way to the taxi rank and joined the queue. She'd have to trust that the driver would know a suitable place. Whilst waiting, she looked around at the bustling city. It was the strangest feeling being in London, with absolutely no one knowing she was there. At least Daniel wouldn't be able to find her, if he was even trying. He was probably drunk. Her heart ached for him. *Oh Lord, please be with him.*

A black cab pulled up in front of her. The driver, a short jolly looking, middle aged man wearing a brown flat cap, got out and helped with her bag, she assumed because of her 'condition', as she hadn't seen any other drivers do this.

"Where to, Madam?"

The question she'd been dreading. *Where to, indeed?* Lizzy straightened herself and gulped.

"I'm really not quite sure…" She looked into the cab driver's friendly eyes and relaxed a little. "Would you be able to suggest a hotel near here that's not too expensive?"

"Sure, I can help with that. I think I know just the place." He smiled and closed the door before climbing into the driver's seat.

Lizzy watched the lights of London flash by without really seeing them. *What was she doing here?*

Safely inside the small but comfortable room at the Great Northern Hotel, Lizzy placed her bag on the rack and took off her jacket and scarf. She rubbed her back as she stood at the window, looking down on the busy road below. It had been a long day. Too long. She needed a shower. She turned and pulled her nightgown out of her bag and headed to the bathroom. As the warm water from the shower flowed over her body, Lizzy marvelled at how God had provided for her. First Scott, and then the cab driver. She closed her eyes and the tension of the day was washed away.

MAYBE IT WAS the unfamiliar bed or the noises of the city, or just because Daniel wasn't beside her, but Lizzy had trouble sleeping. Daniel dominated her mind. All she could do was pray for him, but her heart was heavy as she imagined him coming home to the empty apartment. Did he expect her to be there? Did he expect her to keep her word? Maybe he hadn't even come home. That was more likely.

Morning finally came. How easy it would have been to stay in bed all day, to hide from the world, but she had phone calls to make, so she got up. Sitting on the edge of her bed, her hands shook as she dialled the school's number. In some ways, this was the easiest of all the calls. When the school's receptionist answered, she asked to be put through to the principal. Maybe he wasn't there yet. Lizzy closed her eyes and breathed deeply. She could do this. She had to do this.

"Elizabeth. This is unexpected," the principal said when Lizzy explained she wouldn't be coming in that morning, or anytime soon.

"Yes, I know. I'm so sorry for the short notice, Harold. Family problems. I don't expect to be back before the end of term, and then I'll be on maternity leave. I'm so sorry to do this to you."

One down. Two to go.

Lizzy then dialled Nessa's number. She'd be busy with the children, but she had to be told. How bad would it be if she found out through someone else?

Four rings. Would she answer?

"Hello." Nessa sounded as if she'd been running.

"Nessa. It's Lizzy."

"Lizzy. Are you alright? You don't sound good."

Lizzy gulped and held back her tears. "Yes, kind of." She sniffed and took a breath. "I've left Daniel."

Nessa's exclamation of shock flowed through the phone.

"Not forever, God willing." Lizzy closed her eyes and felt for her cross. "Just until he sorts himself out."

"Where are you, Liz? You can stay here if you want."

"Thanks Nessa, but no, I left yesterday afternoon. I needed to go further away. But can you do me a favour?"

"Sure sweetie. Anything."

"Can you keep an eye on Daniel?" Lizzy wiped her eyes. "I don't know what he'll do. He lost his job, Ness. And he didn't tell me for two weeks." She burst into tears.

"Oh Lizzy. You poor thing. I'm so sorry. I wish I could hug you."

Lizzy sobbed, unable to reply.

"Let me come to you. Where are you?"

Lizzy sniffed and took a deep breath. "No Ness. I'll be alright. Just look out for him."

"Absolutely. Stay in touch, hey?"

Lizzy's grip on the receiver tightened. She squeezed her eyes to stop her tears from flowing.

"Okay."

She fell back on the bed and curled into a ball. Her parents could wait.

LIZZY WOKE two hours later with a growling stomach and checked her watch. If she hurried, she could just make breakfast. She dressed quickly, pulled her hair back, and dabbed on a little make-up to cover her blotchy face. The image staring back at her from the bathroom mirror wasn't flattering, but what did it matter? She grabbed her purse and headed down to the breakfast room.

Only two people were there - an older couple who looked up as she entered. Lizzy smiled at them, and then headed straight for the toast and tea. That would have to do. There was very little left that appealed. At least her hunger pangs would be kept at bay for a while.

When the older couple left, her body relaxed. Why she'd been on edge she wasn't sure. Nobody knew her or why she was on her own, but nevertheless, she'd been awkward and self-conscious with them there. She poured herself another tea and drank it slowly, allowing the sweet warm liquid to revitalise her.

The main dilemma now was whether to stay another night, or go straight home. The prospect of facing Father answered the question. She'd stay another night, and go tomorrow morning. That way, there was no need to telephone until later.

A day in London. No point shopping. She couldn't carry anything. Maybe she could pretend she was a tourist, and just wander around. Catch a bus. Walk through Hyde Park. Maybe even go to the theatre if she could get a ticket. She'd always wanted to see 'The Mousetrap'. But could she do that guilt-free when she'd abandoned her class and had no idea what Daniel was doing, or even if he was okay?

Lizzy's body sagged. Would it be like this the whole time she was away from him? Hadn't she asked God to look after him and do whatever was necessary in his life to make him face his problems? Yes, so what was the problem? Lizzy swallowed the painful lump in her throat. *The problem was her.* She had to let go and trust God. But could she? She wrapped her hands around the still warm cup and leaned back in her seat. *"Okay God, teach me to trust You. I'm sorry for asking You to look after him and then worrying about him straight away. I need to learn how to do it. Please teach me."*

With a much lighter heart, Lizzy returned to her room and prepared for her day out.

LONDON PUT on a lovely autumn day for her. Warm enough to not be bothered with a heavy coat, Lizzy enjoyed the freedom of wandering around the city she hadn't visited for many years, and never on her own. The experience was liberating. Later that afternoon as she sat in the upper circle of St Martin's Theatre, she immersed herself in Agatha Christie's suspenseful murder mystery, and was shocked, along with the rest of the audience, when the murderer was finally revealed.

Maybe she could stay another day... *no, that would be decadent.* She was really just putting off that phone call. Lizzy caught a bus back to the hotel and arrived in time for dinner, and then headed to her room where she took a shower. Her feet ached and her body was tired, but she'd had a great day.

Making that call would spoil it. Could she put it off until the morning? Yes, she'd do that. She'd watch some television tonight, and get up early. With that settled, she leaned back on her bed and flicked on the television.

EVEN THOUGH HER room was on the third floor, the rumble of traffic below was enough to waken Lizzy the following morning. Peering out the window, the grey clouds that filled the sky made her thankful for the lovely day she'd had yesterday. She sat up straight and grabbed her Bible. She needed to stay close to God. Daniel was constantly on her mind, and she longed to know where he was. Had she done the right thing? How easy it would be to forget the reasons for leaving now she was away from him. *'God, please help me stay strong. It's less than two days, and already I want to go back. I know that would be foolish, so please give me strength and wisdom, and please work in Daniel's life.'*

She read a few chapters, and then spent some more time in prayer before taking a shower and preparing for the day. As she brushed her hair, she glanced at the telephone beside the bed. Her chest tightened. Why was it so hard to make this call? If only Sal was home. She closed her eyes and breathed deeply. Maybe it'd be better just to turn up and tell them face to face.

With that decided, she went to the dining room for a quick breakfast before checking out.

CHAPTER 3

*D*aniel couldn't believe it. Who did she think she was? Telling him to sort himself out. *How dare she!* She's the one who needs sorting. He slammed the door as he left and thumped the wall of the staircase. He'd show her. He found the car and sped off. Maybe Johnno would still be at the pub.

He checked his watch and thumped the steering wheel. Too late. He'd have to wait until the next session. He'd go to Johnno's place instead.

Pulling up outside the run down semi-detached several minutes later, Daniel turned the ignition off and leaned back in his seat. He lit a cigarette and turned the radio up. What was she up to? Would she really leave him? He took a long, slow drag and held his breath before exhaling. *It was that big, fat cow of a woman.* If she hadn't dobbed him in, he'd still have his job, and everything would still be sweet with Lizzy. He held his head in his hand. The throbbing was getting worse… his head felt like it would explode any minute. He needed a drink.

Daniel opened the car door and headed inside. He poked his head into the living room, drawn there by the haze drifting out into the hallway. "Danny, brother, come on in." Johnno sat with four, maybe five others, some on the floor, others sprawled on the couch. Bob Dylan played in the background.

"Whad'ya do with your missus?" Johnno clapped his arm around Daniel and handed him the bong.

Daniel lit the cone and inhaled deeply, allowing the magic weed to calm his head before he answered. "She kicked me out. No. Not true. She said she was leaving, so I left first." He snickered and leaned back on the couch. "Have you got a drink, Johnno?"

"I'll get you one, Danny. We'll drink to your freedom, hey boys?"

Daniel grinned at his mate, but his heart was heavy.

∼

NESSA RACED to the door when Riley turned his key in the latch late Monday afternoon. She was still in her pyjamas but she didn't care. She'd been pacing and praying all day, ever since Lizzy's call that morning. Several times during the day she'd considered looking for Daniel herself, but then better judgment stopped her, and she returned to pacing. But now Riley was home, they could take action.

Immediately he walked in, she grabbed his arm.

"We've got a problem, Riley. Lizzy's left."

Riley stood still and tilted his head, eyebrows raised. "She's left? What do you mean? Where's she gone?"

Nessa sighed heavily as she shook her head. "I don't know. She wouldn't say. But she asked us to look out for Daniel." Nessa grabbed Riley's arm tighter. "I feel so bad. We should have warned her about him. It's our fault, Riley. What are we going to do?"

Riley hung his coat on the hook and loosened his tie. "Calm down, Ness. Do you know what made her leave?"

"She said Daniel lost his job two weeks ago but didn't tell her. I think she had enough. She said she needed to go away so he could sort himself out."

"Well, that's not such a bad thing then, if it makes him wake up to himself. Depends on how much he wants her." Riley stepped around her and headed towards the living room. "Let me have some dinner then I'll go look for him." He fell onto the couch as two noisy toddlers jumped on top of him.

∼

BEFORE HE LEFT, Riley stood in front of Nessa and gazed into her eyes. How lucky he was to have her. If it hadn't been for her, he could well be where Daniel was today. Yes, they probably should have warned Lizzy. Now it was their duty to help them. First, he needed to find Daniel.

He brushed Nessa's hair with his hand. "I don't know how much luck I'll have, even if I find him. But I'll do my best. I promise." He leaned forward and kissed her gently before opening the door and leaving.

"Lord God, You need to direct me. I need your wisdom. Please

forgive us for not warning Lizzy. Be with her and give her Your strength. Comfort her, Lord Jesus. She must be really hurting right now. And Lord, be with Daniel, wherever he is. Please work in his life and bring him to Yourself. And use me in whatever way you will, Lord. You know I'm your servant. I'm sorry for failing You so often, but Lord, I'm Yours. You know that. Thank you for saving me, and for bringing Nessa into my life. I'm forever grateful. Thank you Lord."

Riley turned the key in the ignition and drove to 'The Hairy Hog'. As he pulled into the car park, he kept an eye out for Lizzy and Daniel's Ford Escort. He assumed Lizzy had taken it, but didn't know for sure. No, not there. He climbed out of the car and walked around to the front door. What was it about old pubs? They all smelled the same. How many years had it been now? And yet, if he had even one drink, he'd be a goner. He steeled himself and pushed the door open.

Being a Monday night, the bar was quiet. Only a few regulars by the look of it. An old joker who looked like he lived there, poor old sod. A couple of workers on their way home, another one or two in the corner. No Daniel.

He sat on a stool and ordered a squash, not caring what they thought. It was unlikely the young bar maid who'd served him would know, but no harm in asking.

"Looking for a friend of mine. Irishman. Dark hair. Laughs a lot. Seen him lately?" She continued drying glasses, but looked up at him. Her long dark hair made her pale face look even paler. What was a good looking girl like her doing in a joint like this? Surely she could find herself a better job. Riley sighed inwardly.

"Maybe. Think he was here yesterday." She stopped wiping

and leaned on the counter. "I think the guy you're talking about got hauled out by his lady."

"Mmm. So, he hasn't been here today?"

"No, sorry. Haven't seen him, or his mate Johnno. He's normally a regular. Surprised he's not here."

Johnno. Of course.

"Thanks Love." Riley skulled the rest of his squash and gave her a tip as he jumped off his stool.

RILEY CLIMBED BACK into his car and sat for a moment, trying to remember where Johnno lived. He'd only been there once when he'd dropped Daniel off not long after Daniel had arrived in town. Riley knew the area, so he started the car and drove, praying he'd find the place.

He turned his lights on, and headed slowly along Wellington Parade, peering down each street as he passed, but they all looked the same. He turned down Bradley Street and drove slowly between the cars parked on either side. None of the houses stood out. He stopped at the next intersection and peered both ways. More of the same, but maybe this was it. Indicating right, he turned into Kingston Street. The Chippy on the corner looked familiar. And there's the Escort. *Yes, this is it.*

The first available spot to park was fifty yards away. After squeezing into it, Riley stood on the pavement and looked around, thankful he and Nessa had been able to settle in a better area. The houses were tiny, and on the whole, run down, with front gardens overgrown with weeds taller than any of the plants that were hardy enough to survive. He walked back along the pavement towards the Escort, checking each house as he passed.

The semi-detached the Escort was parked in front of looked familiar. Nothing really distinctive to make it stand out, but surely it was the one. He paused before entering, taking a moment to pray, both for himself and for Daniel. What state would he be in?

Riley walked to the front door and knocked. No answer. He knocked again, this time a little louder. The door opened slowly, and Johnno poked his head out. His long straggly hair looked like it could do with a wash, and dressed in faded baggy jeans and an off white T-Shirt with a peace sign on the front, he looked like a left over hippy.

Johnno stood and peered at Riley, a confused look on his face.

"Riley. Come in, man." Johnno opened the door wider and extended his arm. "Guess you're looking for Danny. He's in here."

Johnno led Riley into the living room where Daniel lay on the couch, hands behind his head and eyes closed. A bong sitting on the coffee table looked like it'd been used recently.

Riley stood in the doorway and sighed despondently. *At least he's not drunk.* He walked over to the couch and leaned down and gently shook him. "Hey Daniel. Wake up."

Daniel sat slowly and steadied his bloodshot eyes on Riley. "Hey man. What are you doing here? Sit down." He indicated the spot beside him. A grubby throw covered the couch, and an array of assorted cushions and pillows were scattered both on the couch and on the floor. Riley sat, but declined the offer of a cone.

"So Daniel … I believe Lizzy's gone."

Daniel hung his head.

"Yeah. I stuffed up big time."

"Don't you want her back?"

"She won't come back." Daniel lifted his head and found Riley's eyes. "I'm no good for the likes of her."

"You're right on the ball there, mate, with the state you're in. Look at yourself." Riley shook his head and sighed heavily. "Ness and I had hoped you were past all of this." He glanced at the bong and then back at Daniel, who smelt like he hadn't washed in days.

"I'm sorry, Rilo. I'm a failure." Daniel turned to Johnno. "Can you get us some food, man? I've got the munchies big time." He looked back at Riley. "Do you want something to eat?"

"No thanks, mate." Riley stood up. "Come back with me, Daniel. Ness and I will help get you sorted. It's not too late to get Lizzy back."

Daniel slumped and shook his head despondently. "Nuh. She's gone." His stare was directed at the pile of records sitting on the floor opposite him.

"Well, let me know if you change your mind. I'll drop by again later in the week, and we can talk about it more then. Try to stay off the weed, man. It's no good for you."

Riley walked back out to his car with a heavy heart. It was going to be a long road home.

CHAPTER 4

*L*izzy hailed a cab to take her to Paddington Station. If only another Scott would appear on the scene to help with her bags, but everyone seemed to be in a hurry and took no notice of her. After buying her ticket, she checked the board. Fifteen minutes before the train was due to leave. Not long really. Not long enough to grab a coffee, especially with more stairs to tackle. Her chest was heaving by the time she arrived on the platform, and she headed straight for a seat where she rubbed her back and took some slow, deep breaths. If only Daniel hadn't taken the car.

She looked up as the train came into view. Only a few more hours and she'd be standing on her parents' door step. Lizzy stood and looked for her carriage. Relieved it was only a short walk, she picked up her bags and headed slowly towards the door.

"Here, let me help you with that." She turned and looked at

the tall, dark haired gentleman dressed in a navy suit carrying a brief case reaching out for her bag.

"Thank you very much." Lizzy smiled warmly at the man and accepted the offer of help gratefully.

"My pleasure. Let me put it on the rack for you as well."

God had once again provided for her, and she was thankful.

LIZZY TRIED TO READ, but with every station the train passed bringing her closer to her destination, there was no way she could concentrate. She really didn't want to face her parents, particularly her father. A heavy knot took residence in her stomach, weighing her down.

She looked out the window at the all too familiar scenery. Clusters of houses, and horses grazing happily despite the damp weather, dotted the green rolling fields that resembled home-made patchwork quilts. Small villages centred around churches with steeples visible before anything else came into view. Grand old manor homes perched on hillsides, displaying the prosperity of their owners.

Too quickly the train slowed for her stop. Lizzy stood, and was relieved when the same gentleman once again offered to help. A pity he wasn't getting off here.

Standing on the platform a few moments later on her own, Lizzy determined to carry her own bags the rest of the way. There didn't appear to be as many steps, and besides, she couldn't rely upon strangers all the time. She could do this. It would help build the courage needed to face her parents.

She pulled her shoulders back and stood as straight as she could before making her way down the stairs and through the subway. A young girl with long straggly hair playing a guitar caught her attention, and she dropped a few coins into the girl's hat as she passed.

She hoped her own guitar would still be in one piece when she returned. If Daniel got really angry, that might be the one possession he'd take revenge on. She sighed and continued walking. There was nothing she could do but pray. It was only a guitar when all was said and done, and could easily be replaced.

Two taxis waited at the rank. She gulped and fought the fluttery feeling in her stomach. This was it. The final leg of the journey.

"Where to Ma'am?" The jollier of the two cab drivers walked towards her and reached for her bag.

"Wiveliscombe. Do you go that far?"

"Yes Ma'am. No problem. To a hotel there? Or visiting friends or family?"

Lizzy winced inwardly. Just her luck to get a happy chatty driver again. "Family. My parents own Wiveliscombe Manor." The driver lowered his head and raised his brow just enough for Lizzy to notice. She was sure he would have whistled if it wasn't inappropriate.

Sitting in the back of the cab, Lizzy clutched her handbag the whole way. The closer she got, the faster her heart raced.

As THEY REACHED the gates to the manor, Lizzy leaned forward and instructed the driver to go through and drive right to the house.

Had it only been a month since she and Daniel had driven

up this same driveway? It seemed so much longer. She shivered at the memory of that night. The night he beat her. Maybe it was good to have that memory. Although she'd forgiven him, it helped justify her decision to leave, and to remain resolute in her decision not to return until he addressed his issues.

The few seconds it took to reach the house weren't long enough. Lizzy wanted to tell the driver to turn around and take her back, but before she could, he'd jumped out and opened the door and that option was gone. She breathed deeply and stepped onto the gravel which crunched under foot. The driver lifted her bag out of the boot, and placed it under the portico in front of the double wooden doors. She thanked and paid him. Her mouth went dry as he drove away.

THE ROSE GARDENS either side of the driveway caught her attention. The bushes, heavy with blooms of gold and crimson and salmon were putting on a dramatic display in defiance of the winter chill threatening to extinguish their flame. Lizzy breathed in the heady scent and tried to calm her pounding heart.

The click of the door made her jump. With her hand to her chest, Lizzy turned and looked straight into the eyes of her mother.

"Elizabeth! What are you doing here?" Gwyneth hurried towards Lizzy and threw her arms around her daughter.

Tears streamed down Lizzy's face. She couldn't help it. All that pent up emotion flowed out of her uncontrollably as she was comforted by her mother.

GWYNETH HELPED Lizzy into the house, and led her to the summer drawing room. Seated in front of the bay windows with a view of the rose gardens, Lizzy composed herself. She had to explain her unexpected appearance and uncontrolled emotion. It wouldn't be easy, but at least her mother was on her own.

Lizzy breathed deeply and clenched her hands.

"I suppose you might have guessed already, Mother." Lizzy looked up and held her mother's gaze as she fiddled with her wedding ring. "I've left Daniel." The words she'd never wanted to say to her parents stabbed at her heart. Lizzy forced back the tears that threatened to flow again.

"Oh darling." Gwyneth stood and moved quickly to Lizzy, placing her arm around Lizzy's shoulders. "I had hoped this would never happen."

Lizzy sobbed, her heart at breaking point. "I hope it won't be for long, Mother. Only until Daniel sorts himself out."

"Oh my poor girl. Do you really think he will, Elizabeth?" Gwyneth stroked Lizzy's hair with her free hand, as Lizzy tried to control herself.

"I hope so, Mother."

"I know your father would be pleased if you just forgot about him."

Lizzy pulled back, "Oh Mother, no, I can't do that. I love him. And he's the father of this baby." She looked down and hugged her stomach. "I couldn't do that to him. I'm confident he'll sort himself out. I just don't know how long it will take." She jumped a little and moved her hand to the side of her stomach, and then smiled shyly at her mother.

"The baby just moved. Would you like to feel it?"

Gwyneth hesitated, but then nodded, a faint smile showing on her face. Lizzy gently guided her hand to where she'd felt the movement, and looked into her mother's eyes expectantly as they waited for another movement. Lizzy's smile grew wider as her mother's eyes widened and glistened.

They sat together in warm silence, and for the first time in a long time, Lizzy felt close to her mother.

CHAPTER 5

"*W*hen will father be home?" Lizzy asked her mother as she and Gwyneth sat in the sun room drinking tea.

"He's away on business for the night, so he won't be back until tomorrow evening."

Lizzy let out aa huge breath, and her body relaxed. "I'm not looking forward to seeing him, but at least I've got another day to prepare."

"He's not that bad, Elizabeth. He really does love you."

"He's got a funny way of showing it." Lizzy stood and walked to the window. The clouds had cleared and the late afternoon sun cast shadows over the fields, throwing a yellow tinge over the whole vista. She glimpsed a rider on a horse in the distance bobbing up and down. It'd be nice to go for a ride, but now wouldn't be the right time. She caressed her baby, and wondered what Daniel was doing.

"I'll get your bags taken up to your room," Gwyneth said as she joined Lizzy at the window.

As Lizzy sat on the bed, she recalled the last time she'd been in this room. Daniel had been so angry with her father that night. *Why couldn't he have just let it go?* She fingered the heavy brocade bedspread her mother had bought when she was ten as her mind drifted. Things might have been so much different if they hadn't come that day and had gone straight to Sal's instead. But they had come, and she couldn't turn the clock back.

She'd call Nessa in the morning for any word on Daniel. In the meantime, she needed to unpack.

"You look nice, dear." Gwyneth looked up as Lizzy came downstairs a little while later. Wearing a light blue smock with herringbone embroidery on the bodice and a pair of white maternity slacks, Lizzy was self-conscious under her mother's watchful eye. "You must have bought a whole new wardrobe."

"Kind of. Nessa, that's Daniel's cousin, lent me some of her maternity clothes, so I didn't need to buy everything." Lizzy took a seat on a stool at the breakfast bar as Gwyneth peeled some potatoes. "Can I help?"

"No, but thanks for asking, dear. I wasn't going to bother cooking for myself, but now you're here, I thought I should." Gwyneth put down the peeler and walked to the sink. Her dark brown hair was done neatly in a bun as it had been for as long as Lizzy could remember, but the tinge of grey was new.

"It was a shock seeing you at that door, Elizabeth. I'm glad you came, though." Gwyneth wiped her hands on a towel and then walked back to where Lizzy was seated before placing her hand lightly on Lizzy's shoulder. "Are you really alright, Elizabeth?"

Lizzy lifted her head and looked into her mother's eyes, and for the first time in a long time she saw the mother she remembered from childhood. The mother who she'd snuggled up to every night as she listened to the Bible stories Gwyneth read to her and Jonathon, the mother who waged battle with Lizzy's unruly hair every morning before school, and the mother who used to hug her and make her feel loved.

Maybe she hadn't changed that much after all.

Lizzy shrugged and tried to hold back the tears that welled up behind her eyes. "It wasn't meant to be like this. Daniel is a great guy, he's just got a few problems. I'm praying he'll sort them out and I can go back before the baby comes."

"And what if he doesn't?"

Lizzy's mind raced. She hadn't really thought that far. *No, he had to sort himself out. There was no option.*

She held her mother's gaze. "He will. I'm sure of it."

"Your father won't want you to go back. I'm sure of that."

"What's with Father? Why is he so horrible to everyone?"

Gwyneth walked back to the counter, and picking up a knife, began to slice the vegetables. "He's a hard man to understand, Elizabeth, but most of what you see is just a front. He worries too much what people think, but that's because he's never felt as if he belongs here. You know he got left this estate by a distant relative?" Gwyneth stopped slicing and looked up.

Lizzy nodded and encouraged her to continue.

"Well, what you probably don't know is that before he inherited the estate, he had very little. No job, no money, no name. His parents lived in the poorest part of Exeter, and worked at whatever jobs they could find. His father signed up for the war, but came home a broken man. He took up drinking and became a recluse. Your father left home soon after. Both his parents died within a few years of each other."

Gwyneth walked over and picked up the kettle. "Another cup of tea?"

"That would be nice, thanks Mother."

"Your father was only twenty-three when his great uncle Sydney died and left him the estate. He didn't really know the man. He'd only met him once or twice when he was young, but Sydney had never married, and had no family apart from your father. When your father came to live here, he had to learn the ways of the privileged very quickly, but he's always felt like an outsider, trying to justify his position. He still feels like that, although he hides it well.

Lizzy took the hot tea from her mother and took a sip.

"That explains a lot, but not why he's so distant from us. You'd think he'd relax when he's at home.

"I think he's tried so hard to be someone he's not, he's forgotten who he is." Gwyneth wore a faraway look on her face, and Lizzy's heart went out to her.

"That must have been difficult for you, Mother. I know it was for Jonathon and me growing up. It still is."

"Oh, I've just come to accept that's the way he is." Gwyneth returned to her vegetables.

Lizzy looked up and tilted her head. "How did he get the name, 'Walton-Smythe'? Surely that wasn't his parents' name?"

"Ah yes. I always wondered when you'd ask about that. When your father inherited, his last name was just plain old 'Walton', but Sydney's last name was 'Smythe'. Your father thought if he combined the two, he'd have a better chance of being accepted, so he changed his name by Deed Poll."

Lizzy chuckled, and her eyes lit up. "Funny that. You know I went by plain 'Miss Walton' at school?"

Gwyneth shook her head and looked up, knife in hand. "Really? Why did you do that?"

"I would have been given a really hard time by the other teachers and most of the children if I'd kept my full name. You don't know what it's like up there, Mother. It's a different world."

"I guess I don't." Gwyneth put the knife down and looked Lizzy in the eye. "Elizabeth, what was the real reason you chose to move up there?"

Lizzy gulped and looked away. This was getting a bit too close to home now.

"You don't have to tell me if you don't want to." Gwyneth tilted her head. "But did it have something to do with Mathew Carter?"

Lizzy swung her head around. How had her mother guessed? She sighed with resignation and nodded. "Yes. It was mainly because of him. I couldn't get over him, as much as I tried, so I thought the further away I could get the better. It drove me crazy being in the same town as him, and seeing him almost every other day. I had to go."

"Do you regret it?"

Oh God. How do I answer this? Since when has my mother asked me such personal questions? Lizzy folded her arms and leaned back on the stool.

"I sometimes wonder what would've happened if I'd stayed. I probably would've been sent to a local school, and I'd still be pining after him." Lizzy rubbed the back of her neck and inhaled deeply before looking up. "He still hasn't got another girlfriend, you know."

"No, I didn't know that."

Lizzy glanced out the window and reined her thoughts in before turning back to her mother.

"To answer your question - I needed to get away, so no, I don't regret it. I just wish he'd never broken it off." Lizzy's voice wavered as she spoke.

"You poor girl. I had no idea it had affected you so much." Gwyneth's gentle caring tone tugged at Lizzy's heart.

"Tell me, dear, did you love Daniel when you married him?"

Lizzy's shoulders dropped. Why was she asking all these questions? How could she answer that?

An awkward silence hung between them.

Lizzy gulped and took a deep breath.

"That's difficult to answer, Mother. If you mean, was he all I ever thought of, and did he turn my night into day, kind of." She paused and looked out the window. "But I think, no, I *know*, I would have chosen Mathew over Daniel if I'd had the choice. I didn't, so I chose to love and marry Daniel." Was she really saying this to her mother? How could this be?

"Love is something you choose to do, so I'm learning, even when you don't feel like it. But I'm guessing you know all about that?" Lizzy lifted her eyes and looked directly into her mother's.

Gwyneth had tears in her eyes. Lizzy had been right. Her mother had chosen to love her father, despite everything. Lizzy leaned forward and reached out her hand to her mother, as tears welled up in her own eyes.

"Look at us! What a pair! Just as well Father's not coming home tonight." Lizzy pulled a tissue out of her pocket and wiped her face, as her mother reached for the tissue box on the kitchen bench and did the same.

"How did you get to be so wise, Elizabeth?"

Lizzy frowned and shook her head. "I'm not wise. I've made some really stupid decisions."

"We all have, Elizabeth." Gwyneth drew in a long breath, and straightened herself. "You're a strong girl. It won't be easy, but if you've chosen to love him, that's half the battle."

Lizzy's lips tightened. If only that was true. She let out a breath.

"Maybe you're right, Mother. I hope so." Lizzy picked up her tea and took a sip. "I wonder what Daniel's doing now?"

"Is there anyone you can call to find out?"

"I asked Nessa to keep an eye on him. I thought I'd call in the morning, but maybe I could call now."

"Go ahead, dear. You know where the telephone is."

CHAPTER 6

The phone rang while Nessa was bathing two year old Cindy and three year Jake. Leaving the children for a moment, she grabbed the phone and answered it, all the while keeping one eye on the shenanigans going on in the bath.

Nessa's eyes widened at Lizzy's voice. "Lizzy! How are you? I've been thinking about you all the time."

"I'm okay, Nessa. Oh, not really. I can't stopping wondering how Daniel is and what he's doing. Have you seen him?"

Nessa glared at the children who'd just tipped water all over the floor and were giggling about it. "Sit down you two! Not you, Liz - Jake and Cindy are in the bath, and they're standing up pouring water everywhere."

"Sorry to have caught you at a bad time, Ness. I can call back later."

"No, it's fine. They're just doing what they normally do. I'm just going to ignore them." Nessa leaned against the door but kept one eye on the two young children. "Riley went out last night looking for Daniel, and found him at Johnno's." She stopped. *How much should she say?* She grimaced as her mind raced through the options. How to tell her without telling her... she gulped before continuing. "He wasn't drunk, but he wasn't quite with it."

"What do you mean? What was he doing?" Nessa cringed at the despair in Lizzy's voice, but wanted to protect her from the truth if she could. Lizzy could do without hearing that her husband was stoned out of his brain.

"Riley said that Daniel thinks you've left for good, but it's just his initial reaction. He's obviously in shock. Give him some time, sweetie. We'll keep a good watch on him, don't worry about that. Hopefully he'll come to his senses quickly - for your sake and the baby's."

"I hope so too, Ness. I feel really bad about leaving him the way I did, but I didn't know what else to do."

Nessa jumped as one of the children poured water on the floor, splashing her. She glared at them, but they just giggled. Why did they always misbehave when she couldn't do much about it?

"You did the right thing, Liz. He needed a shake-up, and if this doesn't do the trick, I don't know what will. So, where are you? I'm guessing you went south?" Nessa grabbed the bath toys out of the bath to noisy cries by the two children.

"I'd rather not say, Ness. Then you won't have to lie to Daniel if he asks. I'll ring every couple of days if that's okay?"

"Yes, poppet. No problem at all. We're both praying for you, Liz. Hang in there."

~

LIZZY TOOK a few moments to ponder Nessa's words before returning to the kitchen. *What did Nessa mean? 'Not quite with it?' What was he doing?* At least Riley had found him. That was something. She'd just have to keep praying, and trust that God would work in his life, *'but sooner rather than later would be good, please God.'*

Lizzy wandered back into the kitchen, only to find that her mother was no longer there. Dinner was in the oven, and smelled good. She opened the back door, grabbed a jacket from the hook, and stepped outside. The sunset had faded to a gentle line of orange on the horizon, and directly overhead, stars were starting to appear in the sky. She pulled her jacket tighter as she breathed in the cool evening air.

So many things to take in. She walked along the path through the vegetable garden and found the seat where Daniel had found her the first time she'd brought him here. The day he'd proposed. It'd been so simple back then. Daniel's exuberant personality had taken her mind off Mathew and helped her forget him. But why hadn't she taken the time to get to know Daniel properly before making such a huge commitment? She was paying the price for that oversight now.

Lizzy sighed and gazed at the darkening sky, its beauty drawing her focus to its creator.

'Oh God, creator of heaven and earth, I come to you with a heavy heart. Please help me. You know I'm committed to Daniel, but I can't live with him the way he is. God, please let him open his heart to you. May he come to know the breadth and depth of your love. Soften his

heart, Lord, I pray. And Lord, do whatever You need in my life to make me a better person and a better wife. Let the fruit of your spirit grow in me, Lord, I pray. I really do want to be like You, but I know I fail so often. Please forgive me and breathe your spirit into my life.'

She paused and gazed at the night sky, now strewn with a myriad of stars glittering and twinkling like polished diamonds, and her thoughts drifted to her parents, and the story her mother had told her. *'Lord, thank you for helping me understand my parents a little better. Help me love my father, and to not get upset with him when he says hurtful things. Help me show him your love. And thanks for my mother. Seems she's a lot stronger than I ever thought she was.'* Lizzy chuckled and her heart softened further as she recalled her mother's tears.

'Oh God, thank you for loving me, and for bringing me into your kingdom. Please give me strength and wisdom for the days ahead. In Jesus' name, Amen.'

As Lizzy continued gazing at the night sky, breathing in the perfume from the lavender growing around the seat, she was at peace with herself and with God.

AFTER DINNER, Lizzy and her mother sat in the main living room together, Lizzy flicking through old photo albums and her mother reading a novel. Duchess, Gwyneth's much loved Persian cat, purred gently on her owner's lap.

Lizzy, leaning on a pile of cushions, tucked her feet under her body and took a trip down memory lane. She smiled at the old black and white photos of her and Jonathon dressed up in their Sunday best outfits when they were only about five or six. Her long white socks with frills around the elastic tops, and the pretty yellow dress with the huge sash around the middle. And her hair! What did she look like! The matching yellow ribbons in her pigtails brought a smile to her face. But even then, Father had been so stern. She studied a photo of him standing with Mother. His face was unsmiling and so hard. How had Mother ever loved him?

Lizzy kept turning page after page, stopping every now and then to take a closer look, and putting one album back and replacing it with yet another and another. As she picked up an older looking one, a piece of note paper poked out between the pages. She opened the album to that page and looked at the photos.

She leaned closer. They were photos of Father when he was much younger, but he was with another woman. And they appeared to be taken in Exeter. She recognised some of the buildings and the surroundings, and there was one taken in front of the same church that she and Sal went to when they were at University. She didn't know her father had gone there. And who was the woman? Lizzy glanced at Gwyneth, but as she was engrossed in her book, Lizzy didn't interrupt her, and kept flicking through the pages.

The photos showed that her father and this woman had been close. And her father looked different. In some of the photos, he was actually smiling. *Smiling!* Had she ever seen him smile? It must have been before he inherited, when he was just plain old Roger Walton.

She fingered the note paper. It had that old world look and feel about it, slightly discoloured and quite thin and fragile.

43

Dare she open it? Even years later, it exuded a slight perfume, suggesting it may have been a note from this woman. Lizzy breathed deeply and her hands shook a little as she carefully opened it. The writing was old fashioned but very neat, and although faded, was just legible. Her heart beat faster as she sat up and began to read...

Dear Roger,

My heart weeps as I write this. I don't even know if I can put into words how I feel, but I'll try. To say I was devastated when you broke our engagement is an understatement.

We had such grand plans, you and I. I loved you so much, Roger, and I thought you loved me. But you changed. Sadly, you're no longer the man I fell in love with and wanted to spend the rest of my life with. Inheriting that estate changed you, and not for the better, I'm sorry to say.

My heart's broken, Roger, and I'm angry with you. I don't understand how you could so easily turn your back on all that we had. I don't think you'll ever know how much hurt you caused by telling me I wasn't good enough to be your wife. How dare you! I pray God will forgive me for my anger, I know it's wrong, but I can't help how I feel.

I beg you to reconsider. Don't throw everything away just because you've come into money.

That's all I have to say. I don't know if I'll ever see you again, Roger. I don't know if I could bare it. I can't believe it's come to this.

Your heart broken ex-fiancee,

Hilary

Lizzy's mouth fell open and her heart beat faster. She re-read the letter, and then looked more closely at the photographs of the woman. No, it couldn't be. *But it was.* It was Hilary Carter. Lizzy bit her lip and her skin tingled. *Her father had been engaged to Mathew's mother.*

Gwyneth glanced up at that moment and Lizzy caught her eye. Did her mother know about this? It was too much to take in. Lizzy's mind raced. Surely Hilary Carter must have recognised her the moment she'd walked in her door all those years ago. The daughter of the man who'd jilted her. Why hadn't she said anything? *Oh goodness. This is major.*

"Are you alright, dear? You look a little off colour".

Lizzy took a deep breath. Her eyes were wide open and she was having trouble controlling her thoughts. She gulped and took another deep breath. "I've just discovered something that threw me a little."

Gwyneth tilted her head, slightly puzzled. "That's your father's album. I haven't looked at it in years." She drew her eyebrows together. "What did you find?"

Lizzy hesitated. Should she tell her mother? Her heart beat faster as she thought about what to say.

She had to say something. Best just get it out. Lizzy took yet another deep breath and lifted her eyes to meet her mother's. "That he was engaged to someone else." She waited for her mother's reaction.

Gwyneth put her book down and sighed, closing her eyes for a brief moment before opening them and looking at Lizzy.

"It all happened before I met your father. He told me he'd been engaged to a girl he'd met at church, but that it all fell apart when he inherited and moved in here. Apparently she didn't want to live here." *That's not what the letter said....*

Gwyneth's eyes had a distant look.

"I always felt he still loved her, and that he'd only asked me to marry him to save face." She looked back at Lizzy. "That's why I asked if you loved Daniel when you married him. I'm glad you said you did. At least there's hope for you."

Lizzy stood and put her arms around Gwyneth's shoulders. "Oh Mother. I'm sure he loves you. He can't still be pining after her all these years."

Gwyneth pursed her lips together and shrugged.

"I'm not sure. I feel like I've been living in her shadow all our married life. I never met her, but he compared me with her all the time when we were first married. Why they broke up is beyond me. He obviously still loved the woman."

"That must have been so difficult for you, Mother. How unfair of Father!"

Lizzy's heart fell. Was that how she was with Daniel and Mathew? She'd never said it out loud, but she'd thought it plenty. How often had Daniel noticed?

"Do you know who the woman was, Mother?" Lizzy gulped. Did she really want to have her suspicions confirmed?

Gwyneth reached for the album and studied the photos before lifting her head.

"A girl he met at church. Hilary. That's all I know." Gwyneth's eyes glistened and her voice wavered. "She must have been an amazing person, though, the way he talked about her."

It must be true. Too unlikely there was another Hilary. The woman must be Mathew's mother. This was too much to take in. Lizzy's heart pounded in her chest. Finally, she found her voice.

"Very strange they broke up, then."

Gwyneth sat straighter and took control of herself. "Yes, I always wondered if there was more to it than he told me. He asked me to go out with him soon after. I really think it was to make her jealous and to save face, but I think he loved her so much she almost became saintlike in his mind. But then he slowly hardened into the man he is today."

Lizzy sat beside Gwyneth and looked at her. "I think the woman is Mathew's mother. Hilary Carter."

Gwyneth's eyes widened and she tilted her head. "Really? What makes you think that?"

"There were photos of them standing outside Exeter Baptist. I remember Mathew telling me that his mother used to live in Exeter before she married. And it looks like her. She's very short, and the woman in the photo is short. I'm sure it's her." Lizzy's head spun, loose ends flying everywhere.

"What a small world we live in. Who would have thought?" Gwyneth grabbed a tissue out of her pocket and blew her nose. "I wonder if Mathew knows?"

Lizzy returned to the couch with the album and take another look. "I don't think so. I'm sure he would have said something if he did." She looked up, her eyes a little brighter. "Maybe I should ask him."

Gwyneth looked at her over her glasses. "Do you think that would be wise, dear?"

Lizzy shrugged and closed the album. "I don't know. But maybe I need to see him anyway to find out the real reason he ended our relationship. I never really believed what he said, and I don't know I'll ever be able to move on properly if I don't know. And I do want to move on, Mother. Especially with the baby coming." Lizzy sighed deeply. "I just hope and pray Daniel sorts himself."

Gwyneth smiled at her affectionately. "You really do love him, don't you?"

Lizzy nodded and lifted her eyes, revealing her answer before she spoke it. "Yes, I do. I do love him, Mother."

CHAPTER 7

*D*aniel woke with a start. His heart pounded heavily in his chest, and his head spun. Awareness of his whereabouts dawned slowly. Then it all came back. *Lizzy's gone!* A wail, full of lament and heartache, rose from deep within his body and escaped in a long, deep moan. Whimpering like a dog that had just been kicked, Daniel curled into the fetal position and hugged a cushion to his chest. If only he could sleep, maybe it would all go away.

Images of Lizzy floated through his mind, tormenting him. Why had he got involved with her in the first place? She was too good for the likes of him. But he loved her. Lizzy was the most beautiful thing to come into his life since he'd lost Ciara and Rachel. And he was going to lose her too. He imagined holding her, kissing her, making love to her. She was doing his head in. He'd never get her back.

Daniel sat and ran his hands through his hair. He licked his lips, but his mouth was dry, and his throat hurt when he breathed. Grabbing the half empty bottle on the floor beside him, he took a mouthful, but winced at the taste of the warm, flat beer. Maybe he should go home. She might still be there. But no. Riley said she'd gone. *Riley.* That's right. He was here. Where's Johnno? He looked around, but the place was empty.

He stood and made his way to the bathroom. Looking in the mirror a few moments later, he jerked his head back, not recognising the face looking back at him. Maybe Johnno had a razor. Opening the bathroom cabinet, he found one, and proceeded to shave off the stubble. If Lizzy happened to be home, he should at least look respectable. Maybe he should shower as well.

Once clean, Daniel wandered into the kitchen to look for food. He opened the cupboards and looked in the fridge. Not much to choose from. *Johnno really needs to do some shopping.* He found some bread and a toaster, and cooked two slices, which he buttered and smothered in jam. There was only beer to drink, so he took one and opened it.

He cleared a space at the table and sat down to eat, but couldn't stomach it. The beer helped, so Daniel tipped the toast in the bin, and took the beer to the living room and flicked on the television. Just reruns of the Royal Wedding and a Faulty Towers episode. He left it on Faulty Towers.

What day was it? He rubbed his hair and tried to remember all that had happened since he'd stormed out of the apartment.

He stood and turned the television off. *Now, where are the keys?* He felt in his pocket. Yes, they were there. Daniel grabbed them, opened the front door and walked outside. Lucky it was still warm, because he didn't have a jacket.

Relieved the car was where he'd left it, he unlocked it and

climbed in. His head was still spinning, so he sat for a few moments to steady himself. Then he turned the key and started the engine.

AT THE APARTMENT, Daniel tentatively opened the door, hoping she'd be there waiting for him, but the emptiness that met him revealed that not only had she left, she'd also taken a lot of her things. A heart wrenching ache settled deep inside of him and almost tore him apart.

Her words came back to him as he pictured her sitting opposite him at the table. *'You need to sort yourself out, Daniel. I'm going away for a while.'* He swayed and reached for the wall before slumping onto the couch.

"Lizzy, I'm sorry. *I'm sorry.*" He thumped the couch and buried his head in the cushions, moaning like an injured animal. Her smell was all around him. On the rug, on the couch, in the cushions. Tears welled in his eyes. *"Lizzy, where are you?"*

He couldn't stay here, not without her. He sat and composed himself. His gaze travelled slowly around the room before he stood and headed to the door.

CHAPTER 8

*L*izzy's body ached and she longed for sleep, but her mind wouldn't rest. About midnight she gave up trying and climbed out of bed. Wrapped in one of her mother's dressing gowns, she tiptoed downstairs, put the kettle on and made herself a cup of tea, which she took into the main living room. She turned on one of the table lamps and pulled a rug over her knees as she settled against the cushions.

The baby was active, digging her in the ribs and making her uncomfortable. Maybe it sensed something was going on. She'd need to call the hospital in the morning and organise her next check-up. How terrible if something went wrong.

She sipped her tea and her mind drifted. So much had changed in such a short time. Had it only been yesterday she'd been in London? It seemed such a long time ago.

And now she'd found out that Mathew's mother had been engaged to her father. *Her father!* It was difficult to imagine them together. She'd have to see Mathew. They had unfinished business. There had to be more to the break up than he'd told her. But what would it really achieve? It wouldn't do anything to help Daniel, well, maybe it would. Getting Mathew out of her skin once and for all would have to make a difference, surely.

'Oh God. *Please settle my brain and calm my spirit. And this baby...*' Lizzy hugged her stomach and waited for another kick. *"Pour your blessings out on this little one, and protect it from harm. And God, please be with Daniel. Let him know I love him, wherever he is.'*

Lizzy put her tea down, leaned back on the cushions and closed her eyes.

~

As GWYNETH WALKED along the hallway towards the kitchen the following morning, she passed the entrance to the living room and stopped, her eyes drawn to the figure asleep on the sofa. Standing in the doorway, her heart ached for her daughter.

She'd been glad, but surprised, Elizabeth had chosen to come home. She'd need to speak with Roger as soon as he arrived. Maybe she should telephone him at the office. Yes, that would be best. Forewarn him, and plead with him to be understanding, if that was possible.

Gwyneth continued quietly along the hallway so as not to disturb Lizzy. When she reached the kitchen, she smiled at Duchess who jumped off her bed, stretched, and began to rub herself against Gwyneth's leg. Gwyneth reached down and scratched the cat behind its ear.

The kettle was still slightly warm. Elizabeth must have made herself a drink. Gwyneth reheated it, and once her tea was ready, carried the cup and saucer into the morning room, placing it on the side table beside her Bible.

Gwyneth breathed in the peace and serenity of the early morning and began her quiet time. She poured her heart out to God, and prayed for her family, especially Elizabeth and the unborn baby. She prayed for Daniel, that he'd sort himself out, and that he'd find peace with God. She prayed for their marriage, that they'd be reconciled, and that they'd learn to love and respect each other. And she prayed that somehow, Roger would remember his roots and become that loving, caring man she'd seen in those photos. *'I know you can do all these things, Lord God. Please bless my family. In Jesus' precious name.'*

GWYNETH LOOKED at the clock on the mantlepiece. Still too early to call. In fact, it'd be best to wait until Roger returned to his office in Taunton later in the afternoon. He wouldn't appreciate being called at the Bristol office.

She peeked into the living room. Elizabeth was still sleeping. *She must have needed it, poor girl.* It was Gwyneth's normal shopping day, but she'd put it off - more important to be here for Elizabeth. She took a coat and a hat off the hook, and opening the door very quietly, went outside to do some gardening.

She wandered around to the rose garden, stopping on the way to inspect the Camellia Sasanqua she'd recently bought at the local nursery. The bush was already covered in soft pink blooms, with even more buds bursting to open. She snipped a couple of the blooms and placed them in her basket. The sun hadn't quite reached the rose garden. Dew sat heavy on the bushes which were doing their best to defy the change in season. Gwyneth began the never ending task of dead heading. She didn't mind. It gave her time to think. And pray.

Time disappeared when she was in her garden, and so she was surprised to see Elizabeth standing before her when she lifted her head.

She wiped her forehead with the back of her hand, and then took off her gloves. "Elizabeth dear. I hope you had a good sleep."

Lizzy's smile lit up her face. "Yes, I feel much better now. Thanks for letting me sleep in, Mother."

"You must have needed it. I'll just clean up and I'll make you some breakfast."

"Oh, no need, Mother. I can look after myself. I think I can remember where everything is." Lizzy let out a small chuckle and her eyes glistened.

"Alright then. I'll come in shortly anyway. It's just about time for coffee."

～

LIZZY STOOD for a moment taking in the beauty of the garden. Sadness took hold of her heart as she remembered that she and Daniel had been planning to look for a house. How much she'd been looking forward to having her own backyard and garden. That wasn't going to happen now. But no use brooding over it, there were more important things to be concerned about, like

Daniel sorting himself out. If he did that, they'd be more likely to get a house anyway.

She turned and walked back inside. Lizzy would have been happy to stay here if it wasn't for Father. But at least now she understood him a little better. But would he understand what she'd done when she saw him later today? Only time would tell.

Lizzy filled the rest of the day with menial tasks such as calling the hospital and washing, but she did spend some time at the piano, playing tunes she thought she'd forgotten, but which came back easily once she began.

Even as she sat and let the music pour through her fingers, Lizzy worried about her Father's reaction, and even more, how Daniel was doing.

LIZZY WOKE from a nap to voices filtering up from the kitchen. *Father.* Her heart beat faster, and although tempted to pull the covers up and go back to sleep, Lizzy got up and went to the bathroom.

She splashed her face with warm water, and brushed her hair before pulling it back into a messy bun. That would have to do. She looked at herself in the mirror and took a deep breath. *'Okay, this is it, God. Please be with me. Give me patience and understanding, even if he doesn't have any.'*

"ELIZABETH. Your mother has just told me. It's about time you left that good for nothing Irishman." Lizzy looked at her father standing in the kitchen and felt nothing but pity for him.

Hiding in there somewhere had to be love and compassion. She'd seen it in the photos with Mathew's mother, but it certainly wasn't evident now.

"Nice to see you too, Father." Lizzy held his gaze, waiting to see if he'd realise how cold his words had been.

"I'm sorry, Elizabeth. How are you?" Roger shifted his weight and crossed his arms. His ever so slight smile appeared forced.

"That's better. I'm fine, thank you Father." Lizzy walked up to him and placed a kiss on his cheek. If it made him squirm, she didn't care.

She glanced at her mother, and drew on the strength she'd gained from their rediscovered relationship.

"I'll make coffee for us all, shall I?" Lizzy looked from one parent to the other, and then busied herself under their gaze, far less confident than she looked. Father was not going to bully her anymore if she could help it.

"So, what did Mother tell you?" Lizzy asked as she handed a tray holding the mugs of steaming coffee to her father. He looked uncomfortable, but took it anyway.

"She said you arrived on the doorstep unannounced yesterday afternoon, and that you'd left Daniel."

"Did she also tell you it wasn't permanent?" Lizzy raised her eyebrows as she took a seat in the sunroom.

"Ah, she did mention something like that." Roger sat stiffly in his chair and glared at Lizzy. "You'd be daft if you went back."

Lizzy shook her head and sipped her coffee.

"I know you don't understand, Father, but I love him, and I do plan to go back. He just needs time to sort some things out."

"Yes, you're right. I don't understand. You could have had anyone you wanted, and you chose him." Roger's eyes narrowed. "You've thrown your life away, Elizabeth. After everything we've done for you, and this is what we get in return." He shook his head in disgust. "First you go off teaching, and then you get hooked up with this good for nothing character, and now you're having his child, I really don't understand." He leaned back in his chair and crossed his arms.

Lizzy dug her fingernails into the palms of her hands. She needed to remain calm and not reply in kind, but it wouldn't be easy. *How dare he talk to her like that!* She took a deep breath and exhaled slowly.

She lifted her chin and held his gaze.

"I'm sorry you feel that way, Father. It'd be nice if you respected my decisions for once, and allowed me to be myself instead of forcing me to be someone you want me to be." She paused and slowed her breathing before continuing. "I'm not a child anymore. I know I've made mistakes, but isn't that how you grow and learn?"

Lizzy tilted her head and her voice softened. "I don't believe I've thrown my life away. Just because I don't want to live how you want me to, doesn't mean I'm any less a person. I'm learning more each day about who I am. About who God wants me to be. I wish you'd be happy about that."

There. She'd said it. She held his gaze and waited for his response. Lizzy remained perfectly still waiting for his response. She hardly dared breathe or move a muscle. Her mother also sat still and upright. Such a different person when Father was around.

"Well, it certainly sounds like someone's got in your ear,

Elizabeth, and filled your head with all this nonsense. Why you'd choose to throw away all this is beyond me."

"Father, if that's how you choose to live, I respect that. But I don't want it for myself. Maybe one day in the future I might, but for now, I want the freedom to be myself, to experience life without having everything done for me. But, can we let all that go for now, and just try to be friendly to each other? Especially if I'm going to be here for a while."

Roger sat back in his chair and pressed his hands together. It must be upsetting for him to hear those words from his daughter, but she had to say them... no longer would she allow herself to be pushed around by him.

When he lifted his eyes, they looked a little less cold.

"I don't agree with what you've said, Elizabeth. I do believe you've made a mistake, but I guess it won't hurt to be civil." He sat forward and picked up his coffee. "How long do you expect to be here?"

"I'm not sure, but I hope to be home before the baby comes." Lizzy considered her father carefully. "Are you looking forward to be grandfather?"

Roger shifted in his seat uncomfortably and crossed his legs.

"I haven't really thought about it." He looked up and caught her gaze. "Are you keeping well?"

At last ... a reasonable question! "Yes, I am, Father. Thank you. Much better of late. I just get tired a lot." Lizzy turned her head as her mother stood.

Gwyneth picked up the tray and started collecting the mugs.

"I'll make a start on dinner, but you two can stay here if you like."

"I'll come and help, Mother. I'm sure Father has things to do." Really, she just needed some space. Speaking to Father was exhausting.

Lizzy followed Gwyneth to the kitchen and relaxed.

"It was brave of you to speak to your father like that, Elizabeth, but I'm glad you did." Gwyneth paused while washing the cups and glanced at Lizzy.

"I had to do it, Mother. I hope I didn't go too far." Lizzy pulled out a stool and took a seat.

"No, I don't believe you did. Maybe it'll cause him to think about his attitudes."

"Hopefully it will, but I'm not convinced. Now, what can I do to help?"

"Oh, it's okay, dear. Dinner's mainly ready. But tell me, have you made any plans?"

"I was thinking of visiting Sal for a few days, but I need to find out if she's back. I need to keep busy, or else I'll go crazy." Lizzy crossed her legs and gazed out the window into the distance where the fading daylight was softening the landscape. She turned back to her mother and fingered the cross hanging around her neck. "It's hard to keep my mind off Daniel. I wish I knew what he's doing."

"Be patient, dear. And stay strong."

Lizzy sighed deeply and gritted her teeth. Her mother was right. *Patience.* How she hated that word.

CHAPTER 9

*D*aniel sat in the car not knowing where to go. He felt like just taking off and driving, with no particular destination in mind. No one would miss him. He could go back to Belfast and look up his mates. No, too many skeletons there. He could try to find Lizzy. She'd probably gone to her parent's place or to Sal's, but fronting up at either place didn't appeal, and what was the likelihood of her coming back anyway? He could go to Riley and Nessa's. But they'd only preach at him. He didn't want any of that.

He could try to find another job. But he'd looked for two whole weeks and found nothing. What would be any different now? No, no use doing that. He could go to the Salvos like Lizzy suggested, but he wouldn't be able to have a drink if he did that. No, that one's out, too. *I'll just go to the pub.*

THE BAR MAID GLANCED up as Daniel entered. He plonked down on a stool in front of her.

"What can I get you?"

"Two pints and keep them coming."

She threw him a sidewise look as she pulled the two beers. She should have got that guy's details. It was going to be a long night.

DANIEL STAGGERED out of the pub. The cold breeze off the river slapped him in the face but did little to lift the fog in his head. He found the car and poked his key at the door. The blasted hole kept moving. Once the door opened he fell in. The roar of the motor startled him, he didn't remember starting it...

How close was that car behind? Daniel got out and looked, and stumbled as he tried to get back in. Pulling himself up, he climbed back in, and put the car into reverse. There was plenty of room. The car took off backwards. He slammed his foot on the brake, but it was too late. The sudden stop jolted him into action, and thrusting the gear stick into first, he took off down the road.

Daniel's heart raced. The lights confused him and it was difficult to make out the lines on the road. He needed to stop. He pulled over and pushed open the door just in time. Once the contents of his stomach had been poured out onto the road, he leaned back in his seat and passed out.

The next morning, he headed for the pub, as he did the morning after that, and the one after that, and the one after that, until he ran out of money.

Several times Riley turned up, trying to get him to go home with him, but he just pushed him away. "Leave me alone, mate. I'm no good to anyone. Let me be."

He got into some fights, once with Johnno, once or twice with some old drunks who hassled him for money. He drank more to stop the pain that racked his body and his heart. He slept in the car, in fact, he didn't even bother driving it anywhere. He just slept where it was, parked on the side of the road. Images of Lizzy floated through his sub conscious from time to time, but whenever conscious thought entered his head, he drank more to escape from the pain it brought.

~

THE PHONE RANG on Thursday night as Nessa was cooking dinner. She half expected it to be Lizzy, and she was right. Her heart sank. She had no good news to tell her. Riley had found Daniel the night before at the pub, blind drunk. He couldn't talk straight, and refused to come home with him, so Riley had to leave him there. The bar maid had told Riley Daniel had been there the previous day as well. How could she tell Lizzy all of this? But would it do any good to protect her from the truth? Maybe not. It was probably best she knew.

"Lizzy! How are you, poppet?"

"I'm okay. Missing you all. How's Daniel?"

She wasn't mucking around. She must be really missing him. Nessa sighed deeply and sent up a quick prayer.

"He's not in a good way, Lizzy. He's been drinking, and we don't know where he's staying. Riley saw him last night, but he didn't want to come back with him."

"Oh... I'd hoped he might have got some help by now." Nessa's heart went out to Lizzy on the other end of the phone. The poor girl must be doing it tough.

"It'll probably take a while for him to come to his senses, Liz, but we're sure he will. We just don't know how long it'll take. He's in shock, and drinking's his way of dealing with it. He'll come round, but even then, it's going to take a while for him to get clean, assuming he decides to get help."

"But you really think he will?"

"He loves you, Lizzy. But there's a battle going on inside him. I can't promise you anything, but we think he loves you enough to do something about it when he finally hits rock bottom."

"What do you mean? Rock bottom?

Nessa closed her eyes and chastised herself. Why did she say that? She took a deep breath.

"Usually that's how it goes with alcoholics, Liz. Daniel's on a bender, and sometimes they last for days, if not weeks. Often something happens that makes them stop all of a sudden. We just have to pray that whatever happens will make him realise he needs help. Especially if he wants you to come back."

"Oh... I hope he'll be okay, Ness." Lizzy's voice sounded very fragile and she seemed close to tears. "How do you know all of this?"

Nessa stopped stirring the dinner and took a deep breath.

"Because Riley's an alcoholic too."

"But he doesn't drink."

"No, not any more. He's been sober for five years now, but we went through this as well, Liz. That's how I know."

"Oh Nessa. That gives me such hope. If Riley could do it, that means Daniel can too."

"Yes, but everyone's different, Liz. It has to be Daniel's choice. No-one can do it for him. And there's no guarantee."

"But we can keep praying for him. God can do it. God can do anything."

"Yes, but you know He won't force anyone. It still has to be Daniel's choice."

"Nessa, I just want to be with him. It's killing me being away. And it's been less than a week."

"I know, sweetie. But you've got to hang in there. If you come back too soon, you'll only go through it all again another time. Believe me, I know. I left three times. If you stay strong and let it take its course, there's more chance he'll decide to get help and you'll be back before you know it."

"But it's so hard, Ness. I think about him all the time."

"Have you got people around to support you?"

"Yes, kind of. But it's not the same. It's been good talking to you about it, Ness. I wish you could be here with me, but at least I know you understand. That helps."

"We're praying for you both every day, Liz. And Riley's looking out for Daniel. He gave the bar maid his details last night, and she said she'd call if anything happens to him. He'll be okay, Liz. Call as often as you want. I don't mind."

"Thank you Nessa. I'll call again soon."

After Nessa hung up the phone, Lizzy sat down and prayed. *'Oh God, I don't know I'm strong enough for this. Please help me.'*

CHAPTER 10

*L*izzy struggled for days following her phone call with Nessa. The conversation itself played over and over in her mind. No one had ever said that Daniel was an alcoholic before. Yes, it may have been alluded to, but it had never been stated out loud. That cold hard fact was like a blast of arctic air in Lizzy's face, alerting to her to the enormity of hers and Daniel's predicament. Learning that Riley was also an alcoholic shocked her, but provided comfort since he and Nessa had been through similar trials themselves.

Every day Lizzy tried to call Sal. She desperately needed to talk with her friend, and finally this morning Sal answered. She spent a good half hour on the phone, pouring her heart out to her, and was now looking forward to catching up in person later that day.

Lizzy looked up when Gwyneth joined her in sunroom, and smiled warmly at her mother.

"I heard you on the phone earlier, Elizabeth. I assume you were speaking with Sal?"

"Yes, finally. She just got back from Bristol last night." Lizzy put her coffee mug down and relaxed in her seat. "She has to go back to school on Monday, but has nothing planned before then, so I'm planning on going down there today and will spend the weekend with her."

"I'm sure that will do you good, dear. Will you see Mathew while you're there?"

Lizzy picked up her cup of coffee and took a sip, and then wrapped her hands around the cup as if for support.

"Yes, I think I need to. I know it won't change anything, but maybe it'll help me move on once and for all." She glanced out the window and breathed deeply. "He never really gave me a proper reason for breaking it off, and maybe that's why I found it so hard to get over him. I think there's more to it than he told me, especially now it seems it was his mother in those photos."

"You still have feelings for Mathew, don't you?" Gwyneth leaned forward and squeezed Lizzy's hand.

Lizzy gulped and looked away. Tears welled in her eyes and she wiped them with the back of her hand.

"It's okay, Elizabeth. I think I've known all along. But the question is, what are you going to do about it?"

Lizzy turned her head and looked at her mother.

"He doesn't want me, Mother, so there's nothing I can do but let him go. But even if he did, it's too late now." Lizzy looked down at her wedding ring and fingered it. "I know it's over, and I want my marriage to work, but I think I need to see him one more time."

67

Gwyneth tilted her head and pursed her lips.

"As you long as you know what you're doing, dear."

As THE BUS approached the outskirts of Exeter, Lizzy was deep in thought. Did she really know what she was doing? Would seeing Mathew again really help put him behind her once and for all, or would it only stir up all the old feelings she thought she'd almost left behind? And what would Daniel think if he knew what she was doing?

Just the prospect of seeing Mathew again caused her pulse to race, not a good sign. *Oh God, what should I do?*

The bus was pulling into the bus station, so she gathered her belongings and looked out the window to catch a glimpse of Sal. And there she was. Sal could never hide in a crowd with that red hair. Lizzy waved out the window to her, and when the bus finally came to a stop, stood and made her way to the front.

"Sal!" She wrapped her arms around her friend and fought back the tears that came from nowhere. Why did she have to be so emotional all the time?

"I didn't expect to see you again so soon! Here. Let me take your bag." Sal reached out and took the bag from Lizzy, and guided her towards her car. "How are you holding up, Liz? Are you really alright?"

"I think so, Sal. I sometimes wonder how it all happened, but I'm hopeful it'll work out. I'm really missing Daniel, even with everything that's happened. I just hope he gets himself sorted quickly."

"At least he's got Nessa and Riley looking out for him. It

must have been bad for you to have left. I can't believe he didn't tell you he'd lost his job. That's pretty low."

"Yes, I know. I was so angry when I found out. He could have just told me, but no, he hid it from me and then went on a bender." Lizzy's lips compressed into a thin flat line.

"Here's the car." Sal unlocked it and opened the door for Lizzy. They both climbed in.

"Do you really think he's going to change, Liz?"

Their eyes met and Lizzy cringed.

That was the question that haunted her day and night. Would Daniel ever be any different? Could he stop drinking? Would he ever allow God to change him? And if not, would she be able to live with him the way he was?

Lizzy shrugged dejectedly. "I hope so, Sal. I pray for him all the time. But like Nessa said last night, there's no guarantee."

Sal reached out and squeezed her hand. "Chin up, Lizzy. He'd be mad to let you go."

Lizzy smiled weakly and let Sal's words encourage her. Sal always knew what to say.

"SORRY THE HOUSE IS A MESS. I just dropped everything when I got the call about my mum, and Lauren's hopeless with housework."

"It's not a problem, Sal. It doesn't look too bad, anyway."

"Always the diplomat! So, what do you want to do? We've got all weekend to ourselves." Sal turned the kettle on and busied herself making coffee.

Lizzy pulled out a seat and sat at the table. "Maybe some fun things to get my mind off Daniel for a while. Go to the cinema perhaps, but mainly just hang out. I don't really want to see anyone. I couldn't handle all the questions."

"Yes, I guess not. We can hide out here, it's okay, Liz. No one knows I'm back yet." She carried the two coffees to the table and sat down.

"I do want to see Mathew while I'm here." There, she'd said it.

Sal's eyes widened, and her mouth fell open.

"Why, Lizzy? What good will that do?"

Lizzy sighed and picked up her mug.

"I just need closure, Sal. I don't think he told me the truth about why he broke it off. I'm hoping that if I know, I'll be able to put it behind me once and for all, and move on properly. It just nags at me. I know it's over, especially now." She looked down at her tummy and her lip twisted into a sardonic smile. "Maybe it's stupid, but I just need to know. We'd been planning our future, Sal. *We were so happy.* You know that. It's hard to understand why he changed his mind all of a sudden with no real reason. Is that stupid or not?"

Sal squeezed her hand. "No Lizzy, it's not stupid. If it helps you to move forward, you should see him. I can ask him over if you like."

Lizzy flashed her a smile. "That would be good. Thanks Sal. There's one more thing. Take a look at this." Lizzy pulled the photo she'd removed from her father's photo album out of her bag. "Do you know who that is?"

Sal took the photo from Lizzy and inspected it before shaking her head. "I'm guessing that's your father. But who's the woman?"

"It's Mathew's mother."

"No way! Get out of here!"

"I'm pretty sure. I found a letter from that woman to my father, signed Hilary. That's his mother's name. And it looks like her. I don't understand, though, if it's her, why she didn't say anything to me when I stayed there. She must have known who I was."

"Maybe she didn't know."

"She must have. Father broke off their engagement when he inherited the estate, and that's when he changed his name, so she must have known. I want to ask Mathew if he knew."

Sal rolled her eyes.

"You might be opening a bag of worms."

Lizzy leaned back and grimaced.

"I know."

CHAPTER 11

*L*izzy listened as Sal arranged with Mathew to come for lunch the following day. Sal told him Lizzy was in town and wanted to see him, but didn't fill him in on all the details. They'd agreed it'd be best to leave that to Lizzy.

All night, images of Daniel and Mathew flitted through Lizzy's mind, and when the early morning sun peeked through the blinds and woke her, she turned over and went back to sleep. It was close to nine o'clock when she stirred again, and she had a sudden panic attack when she glanced at the clock. Mathew would be here in just over two hours. Her pulse raced at the thought of seeing him again. How would she survive?

She pulled herself up and calmed her breathing before climbing out. It wouldn't do her or the baby any good to be so on edge. She pulled on a dressing gown and headed to the kitchen to make a pot of tea. The house was very quiet. Neither Sal nor Lauren were around.

Lizzy took her tea and piece of toast outside to get some

fresh air. It wouldn't be long before it'd be too cold to sit outside, so best enjoy it whilst she could. How nice it was to have a garden. Sal definitely wasn't a gardener, but still, it was much better sitting out in the sun in a slightly overgrown backyard than in an apartment where you could only look out the window. She sighed and wondered where Daniel was. Was he even missing her? She fought back the tears that threatened to fall, and prayed for him. How long could she stay away? *God, please give me strength.*

She heard a door close and some clanging and banging coming from inside. Sal must be back. Lizzy picked up her mug and plate and headed inside. Sal was unpacking grocery bags, and looked up as Lizzy entered.

"There you are, sleepy head."

"Sorry Sal. You should have woken me."

"No, you looked too peaceful, I didn't want to disturb you."

Lizzy smiled kindly at her. "Thanks. I had a fairly rough night. Couldn't get either of them out of my head."

"Mathew and Daniel, you mean?" Sal glanced up at her.

Lizzy nodded as she washed her mug and plate.

"Yes, they haunted me all night, but they got all mixed up in my dreams. It was really weird." She shook her head and let out a small laugh.

"Are you okay?"

Lizzy stopped and took a deep breath. "I think so…" She put the mug she was wiping down and turned to look at Sal. "No, I'm not alright, Sal. I'm nervous about seeing Mathew. I don't want to make a fool of myself."

"It's not too late to call it off."

Lizzy closed her eyes briefly and steadied herself.

"No, I need to see him, but I need to calm myself before I do."

Sal walked over to Lizzy and wrapped her arms around her, pulling her close.

"I'm sure you'll be fine. Why don't you shower and get dressed while I make a start?"

Lizzy wiped her eyes and nodded. Thank goodness for Sal.

NOT HAVING BROUGHT many clothes with her, Lizzy had limited choice of what to wear. In the end, she decided on a light blue pinafore over her white stretch jeans. Not the most flattering of outfits, but it would have to do.

She couldn't stop checking the clock as she helped Sal with the finishing touches for lunch.

"Will you stop that! You're driving me crazy!"

"What am I doing?"

"You're fidgeting. Sit down and talk to me. Tell me about your holiday."

Lizzy sat and folded her arms. "No, I can't think about that right now."

"Okay, then talk to me about something else. Tell me what you did in London."

Lizzy began to tell Sal about her day or so in London, but stopped mid-sentence as the doorbell rang. She sat up and placed her hands on the table, her gaze meeting Sal's. She inhaled deeply.

"I'll go." Sal took off her apron and placed it over the back of the chair, and squeezed Lizzy's shoulders before walking to the front door.

Lizzy straightened her shoulders and lifted her chin. This wasn't going to be easy. She listened intently as Sal opened the door and let him in. The sound of his quiet gentle voice made her skin tingle. She grabbed the cross around her neck and looked up. *'God, please give me strength.'* She squeezed her hands to her chest, and then stood.

Her pulse raced and her skin went clammy. Could she really face him again? She closed her eyes for a moment and calmed her breathing.

And then he was there. Standing right in front of her. His eyes met hers as he held out his hands.

"Lizzy. So good to see you."

Lizzy reached out and took them, and gazed into those eyes. The years apart slipped away and it was like time had stood still. If only he would pull her close and wrap his arms around her, all would be right. But that would never happen, and it was wrong to even think that way.

"Mathew." She smiled shyly and then tilted her head slightly. "It's good to see you, too. Thank you for coming over." She let go his hands, and moved out of the way to let Sal through.

"I was surprised to hear you were down, especially after seeing you and your husband so recently. But I couldn't refuse Sal's invitation of a free lunch." His eyes sparkled as he grinned at Sal before turning back to Lizzy. "She said you wanted to see me."

Lizzy lowered her eyes and gulped.

"Why don't I leave you two together?" Sal interrupted them. "Lunch is all ready, you just need to serve yourselves. I've got some work to do, so I'll grab a plate and take it to my room."

"Sal… you don't have to leave." Lizzy grabbed Sal's arm. Her eyes were startled. "Stay?"

Sal eyes were firm and she held Lizzy's gaze.

"No, Liz. I really do have work to do, and you two have things to talk about. I'll just be in my room."

Lizzy let go of her arm and glanced at Mathew, who still stood just inside the doorway. What would he be thinking? This wasn't a good start.

Sal took her plate and left the room. Lizzy's heart beat rapidly. She looked up at him.

"I'm sorry Mathew. I wasn't prepared for that. Come and sit down." She took a seat and indicated for him to take the one opposite. Now he was here, she didn't know what to say.

"Would you like a drink?"

The corners of Mathew's mouth curved into a smile.

"It's okay, Lizzy. No hurry. Just relax."

She returned his smile as she breathed in slowly and leaned back in her seat.

"Thank you." Outside the sun shone in the sky with only a few wispy clouds in the distance. "Why don't we sit outside for a while? It's nicer out there."

He nodded agreeably and stood, and then helped her out of her chair.

"Are you keeping well, Lizzy?" he asked as they headed outside.

"Yes, thank you." She hugged her tummy. "Just over three months to go now."

"You must be getting excited."

Lizzy grinned as love for her unborn baby warmed her heart.

"Yes, I am. A little scared, though." Her shoulders fell slightly and she let out a small sigh.

"Is everything alright, Lizzy?" Mathew turned to face her once they'd taken their seat. He was so close, she could almost feel his heart beating beside her. How wise had this been?

Lizzy looked into his eyes and gulped. *Lord, I need you right now. Help me to stay strong.*

"Not really." She proceeded to tell him about Daniel's drinking problem, and how she'd made the decision to leave him until he got help. Lizzy surprised herself, and despite the heaviness in her heart as she spoke about Daniel, her eyes remained dry.

"I do love him, Mathew, and I pray every day that he'll find God and that he'll sort out his problems and we can be together again, but there's something else that's bothering me." Lizzy inhaled deeply and gazed at the garden before turning to look at him.

"What's that?" Mathew tilted his head and looked at her quizzically.

"What was the real reason for our break up?"

Mathew frowned, drawing his brows together.

"What do you mean, Lizzy? It was just as I said."

Lizzy's heart raced and she clenched her hands together to stop them from shaking.

"No, there has to be more. You couldn't have just woken up one morning and thought, *'Lizzy's not the one'*, after all we'd been planning. What didn't you tell me, Mathew?"

Mathew squirmed in his seat and folded his arms.

"It won't change anything," Lizzy said, "I realise that, but Mathew, it haunts me, not knowing. Maybe it shouldn't, especially now I'm married, but don't you owe it to me to be honest?" Her eyes pleaded with him. "You might not be aware of this, but the reason I left was to get away from you. I couldn't handle being in the same town as you. Seeing you in the distance every day or so was driving me insane. I didn't have an option, really. But our breakup changed my life, Mathew, and not knowing why hasn't helped."

He lowered his head and sighed. He remained silent for what seemed an age before looking up.

Lizzy hardly dared breathe. Her heart beat so loudly he must have heard it. Her hands were clammy and her throat hurt when she gulped.

"Lizzy, I'm so sorry for hurting you like that. And yes, you're right. There was more to it." His eyes had watered and a pained expression sat on his face. "I didn't want to break up, Lizzy. Believe me. I loved you, and it was the most difficult decision I ever had to make."

"Well, why did you, then?"

He stared down at his feet and shook his head slowly.

Lizzy held her breath. This was the moment she'd been waiting for for almost three years. What would he tell her? Her heart thumped and her hands began to shake.

He lifted his head and looked into her eyes.

"It was my mother." He gulped and blinked rapidly.

"Your mother?" Lizzy's mouth fell open.

"After your visit, she called me every second day to tell me you weren't the one for me. She was incessant. In the end, I had to decide between you or her." Tears rolled down his cheeks. "I'm sorry, Lizzy."

Lizzy's breathing quickened and she felt faint. Hilary must

have known who she was. But what caused her to dislike Lizzy so much she made Mathew break it off? Lizzy's body shook and she buried her head in her hands. Hilary had never shown any dislike to her the whole time she'd been there. It was too much to bare.

Mathew moved closer and wrapped his arms around her. She sobbed into his shoulder. His heart beat loudly, and she could feel his chest rising and falling. What had they done to deserve this? *Torn apart by his mother.* But why did Mathew choose her instead of Lizzy? Surely he could have stood up to her?

Lizzy's tears subsided and were replaced with anger. Her heart beat faster and she pulled away. She looked at him accusingly.

"Why didn't you stand up for me if you loved me so much?"

Mathew looked crest fallen.

"You don't know her, Lizzy. She might seem quiet and gentile on the outside, but underneath, she's a force to contend with. I don't know why she took a dislike to you, but she said she knew you weren't the one from the moment she met you, and she wouldn't let it go. She made it impossible for me to be with you without thinking of her. It would never have worked."

Lizzy pursed her lips and fought back her tears. This was too much to bare. Why hadn't he stood up for her? He loved her, after all. He'd said so.

"It makes me really sad you didn't fight harder, Mathew. You obviously didn't love me enough." She folded her arms. He had a hurt look on his face. Maybe he'd been suffering too. "But I also don't understand how anyone has the right to tell anyone else who they should or shouldn't be with. It's wrong."

She hesitated before pulling the photo out of her pocket and handing it to him.

"Take a look at this."

Mathew took the photo and held it up. He studied it closely, his eyes widening.

"That's my mother." He pointed to the woman. Then he turned his head and stared into Lizzy's eyes. "That's not your father, is it?"

Lizzy nodded and took a deep breath. Her suspicions had been confirmed. She looked at him intently.

"Did you know?"

"No, I had no idea."

"They were engaged. My father broke it off when he inherited." Lizzy grabbed his arm. "She must have known who I was as soon as she heard my name. I think she turned you against me out of spite."

Mathew jerked his head up. "She'd never do that."

"Are you sure? Did she ever give you a good reason?"

Their eyes locked together and time stood still. If it was true, how could Lizzy ever forgive her for putting Mathew in that situation, for ruining their hopes and their dreams? Did Hilary despise her father so much that she would do this?

Mathew shook his head slowly.

"Maybe you need to go and see her."

He shrugged dejectedly and peered sadly into her eyes. "It's not going to change anything, Liz. It's too late for us."

"But if that's what she did, shouldn't we at least know? It's not right, or honest, if she did. You never know, she might be feeling guilty but hasn't been able to tell you. You'd think that something like that would eat away at you."

"Mmm. Maybe I should. I did ask her why, but she always said it was just something about you, but she really believed she was right, and never wavered." He crossed his arms and narrowed his eyes. "Now I think of it, she did say once or twice she thought being a minister's wife would be too much of a come down for you."

Lizzy's shoulders slumped. That was all she'd ever wanted. To be Mathew's wife, supporting him in his ministry. *How dare that woman take her dreams away!* It wasn't fair or right. "

"I think you need to talk to her."

"Yes, I think you're right, Lizzy. I will. I'll go and see her." He breathed slowly and deeply and his face softened as he gazed into her eyes. "I'm so sorry, Lizzy. I should have stood up to her."

The tears that Lizzy had been holding back now flooded down her cheeks. If only he had, everything would have been different. But it was too late.

She grabbed his hand and held it to her face as he wiped her tears away with the back of his other hand. She had to let go, but she clung on for just a moment longer. As she slowly pulled away, their eyes locked together, and in that moment, all the love they'd held for each other passed between them in unspoken words, but they both knew it was over.

Lizzy took his hand. "Come on, Mathew, let's have lunch."

CHAPTER 12

"We'll always be friends, Lizzy," Mathew said as their gaze lingered on each other at the door. Her knees weakened as he bent down and kissed her gently on the cheek, before turning around and walking away.

Sal wrapped her arm around Lizzy's shoulder as they stood together watching him disappear into the distance.

"Come on, I'll make you some coffee."

Lizzy could hardly stand. Her heart felt like it had been ripped out of her. There could have been no other outcome, but oh, it was so hard to let him go.

She smiled weakly at Sal. "Thank you."

Retreating to the living room with their coffee a few minutes later, they curled up on opposite couches. Lizzy remained quiet for some time, lost in her thoughts. Her heart was heavy. Finally, she recounted the conversation she'd had with Mathew. Talking about it made her feel better, stronger, and slowly, indignation replaced her heart ache.

"It just doesn't seem right, Sal. What makes people, including our parents, think they can control who you marry? Why can't they just respect your choice? Sure, they should be free to say what they think, but in the end, shouldn't the decision be ours?" Lizzy shook her head and sighed deeply. "I just don't understand it. First my father, and now Mathew's mother, I just don't get it."

"I guess they just want the best for their kids, and think they're doing the right thing, but I agree, they shouldn't make it such that you're left with no say." Sal grimaced, and picked up her coffee.

"But they've made their decisions based on prejudices and resentment. Father's so caught up playing the part of an English gentleman he'd never accept anyone who wasn't in the same league. He also thinks all Irishman are good for nothing."

Lizzy sat up and leaned forward. Her body tensed and her pulse quickened. "It's simply not true. And then there's Mathew's mother." Tears welled in her eyes.

"Lizzy, calm down. It won't do you any good." Sal sat up and moved to the couch beside Lizzy and hugged her.

"I know you're angry, but you've got to be bigger than this." She gently stroked Lizzy's hair. "Let it go, Liz. What's done is done, and the most important thing now is to forgive and move on. You've got Daniel and your baby to think of now." She pulled her tighter as Lizzy sobbed into her chest.

LATE AFTERNOON, they went to the cinema, and on their way home, Lizzy told Sal she wanted to go to church in the morning.

Sal raised her eyebrows. "Are you sure? Mathew's preaching."

"Yes, I know." Lizzy took a deep breath. "I feel stronger, Sal. I'll be alright."

"Even if people ask questions?" Sal glanced at her as she parked the car outside the house.

Lizzy took a slow deep breath and pursed her lips. "Yes, I'll deal with it."

"Okay then," Sal said as she opened the car door. "As long as you know what you're doing."

"Not really, but I'm getting there." A faint glimmer of a smile grew on Lizzy's face. "Thanks for everything, Sal." She grabbed Sal's hand and squeezed it. "I mean it. You've been such a good friend to me. I don't know what I would have done without you."

"Come on, Liz, don't get all soppy on me again." Sal's grin was infectious as she threw Lizzy's hand off.

BEFORE SHE WENT TO BED, Lizzy pulled her Bible out of her bag and opened it. She had business to do with God, but was she ready? She'd been cheated, even though she loved Daniel and would return to him. But letting go of what might have been and forgiving those who were instrumental in changing the course of her life wasn't going to be easy.

How different life would have been if she and Mathew had married. She would have been beside him, supporting him in his ministry, and they would have been happily married, without all the issues she and Daniel were having to work through. But maybe they would have had other issues. She'd never know.

The hurt in Mathew's eyes when he'd learned the truth of what his mother had done made her weep. If only he'd stood up to her.

He seemed so lonely. Why hadn't he found someone else? She prayed that God would bring the perfect person into his life, and that he'd be happy. As she prayed for him, her heart lightened. Maybe this was the first step to full healing. Forgiving his mother wouldn't be that easy, of that she was sure.

Before going to sleep, Lizzy picked up the wedding photo she'd brought from home and gazed at Daniel. Such a handsome man, with his cheeky eyes that could light up a room. *Oh Daniel, please sort yourself out. Please.*

She hugged the photo to her chest, and curled up in bed. Sleep came easier that night, with only Daniel occupying her thoughts.

As Lizzy entered the church, her mind was drawn to the last time she'd been there, not much more than a month before, but in such different circumstances. How she longed to have Daniel beside her again. The week apart seemed more like a year, and she just wanted to hold him. She'd try to call him soon, and pray that he'd taken steps to deal with his drinking problem.

But right now, she'd join in worship with Sal beside her, and trust that God would be working in his life. The organ played and they stood to sing the first hymn. Lizzy squeezed Sal's hand and smiled warmly at her. Just like old times.

The moment Mathew stood to commence his sermon, Lizzy held her breath. Would she be able to look at him without her heart racing or her hands shaking? Would his hold over her be finally broken? She looked at him standing behind the pulpit. So confident in a quiet way, and his smile lit his face, exuding warmth and love to the whole congregation. He'd make a wonderful husband for some lucky girl. He caught her eye, and for a moment time stood still. How was it possible that so much could be conveyed through just one look? But Lizzy knew in that moment she'd always love him. Not as a lover or a husband, but as a dear friend.

She breathed deeply and relaxed, and listened intently as he began to speak.

"If we're to walk closely with God, we must forgive. There is no choice. Why? Because Jesus commanded it. As simple as that."

Lizzy's body went goosy. Had the topic been a last minute choice, or had God planned it all along? She shivered, and pulled her coat tighter.

"But how can a person whose heart has been trampled on, and whose emotions are in tatters because they've been wronged by somebody, find it within themselves to forgive that person?"

Oh Mathew, how are you doing this? It must be tearing you apart. Lizzy struggled to control her own tattered emotions.

"How can they let go of the hurt and the anguish caused by this person and not only forgive them as Jesus commanded, but also love them?"

Lizzy closed her eyes and tried to settled herself. The words Mathew spoke were coming straight from God, and it was almost too much to bear.

"Only Jesus can enable us to forgive the one we deem to be unforgivable. It's the forgiveness we receive through Jesus that makes it possible for us to forgive others. True forgiveness acknowledges that a genuine wrong has been performed, and it doesn't belittle the pain that this wrong has caused.

"Instead, forgiveness says, 'although I was truly wronged, I won't allow that wrong to control my life. Although I was deeply hurt, I won't let the hurt fester and harden my heart. Instead, I'll release the wrong, and the wrong doer, and hand them both over to the Lord.'"

Lizzy's heart beat faster. God was speaking directly to her.

"The act of forgiveness is something you choose to do. By allowing the love and grace of God to permeate your heart, you can then live a life free of bitterness and resentment. Rely on God's strength and grace to help you release the person and to love them, with no strings attached.

Let me finish by reading Ephesians 4:31-32, which sums up beautifully how we can be free to love and serve God with all our hearts with our consciences clear: 'Get rid of all bitterness, rage and anger, brawling and slander, along with every form of malice. Be kind and compassionate to one another, forgiving each other, just as in Christ God forgave you.'

Please pray with me today if there's someone in your life you need to forgive. Let's bow our heads.

Dearest Father, thank you for the forgiveness you offer us through Christ. Thank you for the undeserved grace and mercy you pour out on us every day. Thank you for the joy and freedom we experience when we confess our sins to you and in return are forgiven for those sins. And thank you that as we experience your forgiveness, you enable us to forgive others.

But Heavenly Father, sometimes it's hard to forgive. "Yes, it is, God. It's hard." Sometimes the wrongs are so hurtful and the wounds so deep that forgiveness seems almost impossible. Your instruction to forgive is clear, but sometimes we don't have it within us to do so. And sometimes we simply don't want to.

So, loving Father, we ask you for help. May our own experience of your grace and mercy both heal and change us, and give us the courage and strength to forgive, even when we've been terribly wronged."

Lizzy couldn't hold it any longer. Tears she'd been holding back rolled down her cheeks as God touched her heart.

"Today, I pray for those who are struggling to forgive. And Lord, I include myself in that. Open our hearts to your love. May we comprehend the majesty of your mercy. Help us trust you, even to the extent of forgiving those who've hurt us so very deeply that we may not want to forgive. May we know your healing and love in our lives when we follow your example and choose to forgive.

All praise to you, God of mercy and grace, God of healing and love and forgiveness. Amen.' "

LIZZY WIPED her face and remained still with her head bowed. Her heart was pounding. Sal reached out and squeezed her hand. God, through Mathew, had nailed it perfectly. He'd met her right where she was, and challenged her to forgive. To forgive Hilary, her father, Mathew. Yes, she would forgive them, and she'd let go of the hurt and the disappointment she'd been holding in her heart for so long. She'd grasp God's love with both hands, and trust Him to fill her with his peace as she moved forward in His strength.

She lifted her head. She wasn't the only one in tears. God had done a mighty work in a lot of lives. A quiet hush had fallen over the congregation, and instead of the normal conversations at the end of a service, people filed out slowly and quietly.

When Lizzy reached the door and faced Mathew, she held out her hand to him. His eyes were slightly red, and he looked tired. No words were required, but Lizzy had something she needed to tell him.

"There's no need to ask her, Mathew. It's okay. Let it be."

He gave her a beautiful, thankful smile.

"Thank you, Lizzy. I'll pray about it." He looked deeply into her eyes as he gently held her hand. "You take care now." As she withdrew her hand slowly and turned to leave, their gaze lingered for just a second longer than it should before it was broken and she and Sal walked away.

"WHAT A WEEK," Lizzy said to Sal as they walked arm in arm back to Sal's car. "This time last week I was out looking for Daniel. It seems so much longer than that."

"You're missing him, aren't you?" Sal stopped in front of the car and reached into her bag for her keys.

"Yes, I am. I just wish I knew what he was doing." Lizzy tilted her head and sighed wistfully. "I think I'll call Nessa again tonight, if that's okay."

"Sure, no problem, Liz." Sal unlocked the car and they

climbed in. She put the keys in the ignition and then looked at Lizzy. "How about we go somewhere for lunch?"

Lizzy's eyes lit up. "Yes, that would be great! How about we go to that pub we used to go to at Woodbury Salterton?"

"Done. Let's go." Sal started the car and pulled out of the car park onto Wonford Street, before turning right onto Butts Street and then joining the B3183 towards Woodbury Salterton. Being a Sunday, the traffic was light, and it would only take about twenty minutes to get there.

"That was some sermon today," Sal said, glancing at Lizzy as she slowed down for a red light. "I don't think there was a dry eye in the church."

"Yes, it was certainly a powerful message." Lizzy looked at Sal and crossed her arms. "You know, I think Mathew was almost as surprised as I was when he found out what his mother had done. Maybe I shouldn't have shown him that photo, or pressed him for answers. I feel really bad now that I might have ruined their relationship. Maybe I should've just let it all go, and dealt with it myself."

"It's done now, Liz. You can't change it, and really, he did owe it to you to explain why he ended it. Especially when you were so close. I'm sure he'll do the right thing, and you never know, it might make his relationship with his mother stronger."

"Maybe." Lizzy stared out the window, deep in thought, as they drove the last few miles. Had she done the right thing leaving Daniel as she had? Yes, he'd wronged her, there was no question about that, but should she have forgiven him and stayed? Nessa said she'd done the right thing, but after today's sermon, she wasn't so sure.

"Here we are," Sal said as she pulled into the car park of the Diggers Rest a few minutes later. "Full house today."

"I hope they haven't run out of their chicken pies!" Lizzy said, opening her door and sliding out onto the gravel.

"Let me help you, you poor old thing!" Sal ran round to Lizzy's side, but it was too late. Lizzy had already regained her footing and steadied herself.

"I'm not poor and I'm not old, thank you very much!" Lizzy was indignant and pushed off Sal's arm.

"No, but you did have trouble."

"Well, you shouldn't have a car that you need a step ladder to get in and out of."

Sal chuckled as she closed the door and locked the car. "Maybe I'll replace it one day, just for you."

Lizzy shook her head and grinned. "That'll be the day."

"Come on then, let's go get some food before there's none left."

THEY FOUND a table in a cosy corner and ordered their meals. Lizzy ordered the Chicken and Leek Pie and Sal ordered the grilled fish, just like old times. They both ordered a lemon squash.

Lizzy took a sip of hers, and then put her glass down. She leaned forward and rested her folded arms on the table.

"Sal, do you think I did the right thing, leaving Daniel?"

Sal's head shot up. "What brought that on?"

"Oh, I was just thinking after the sermon this morning. Maybe I should have just forgiven him and stayed."

"No Lizzy." Sal reached out and grabbed Lizzy's arm. "He

needed a good wake up call. The way he was treating you wasn't acceptable."

"But I feel like I'm blackmailing him, telling him I won't go back until he gets help." Lizzy leaned back in her seat, her arms still folded. "I don't feel right about it, Sal."

Sal sighed and ran her hands through her hair. "Oh Lizzy. I wish I could wave a magic wand and fix it for you, but I don't think it's that simple. I don't think you're blackmailing Daniel. He might see it like that, but if he loves you enough, surely he'll see that he really does need to get help."

Lizzy shook her head and glanced at the young couple sitting at the next table. They were holding hands and looked so in love. She and Daniel used to be like that. She grimaced and her body slumped.

"Lizzy, you've just got to stay strong. Look at me."

Lizzy turned her head back and lifted her gaze to Sal's.

"You can't go back and put yourself and the baby in danger. I saw what he did to you when you were down here before. If he's done it once, he can do it again, and maybe even worse."

"But he promised he never would." The picture of Daniel lifting his hand to her when she told him she was leaving flitted through her mind. *But he put it down. He didn't hit me.*

"Didn't he promise to talk to you about his problems too?"

Lizzy lowered her head and breathed deeply. *Yes he did.* Why couldn't he have just told her he'd lost his job instead of hiding it from her?

"You can't go back yet, Lizzy. Not until he's done something about it. If you do, you'll be asking for trouble."

Lizzy looked up as the waiter delivered their meals,

thankful for the diversion. She placed her napkin on her lap and picked up her knife and fork.

"Okay, you win. But I'd like to at least talk to him sometime soon."

"Alright. I'll let you do that. Now, let's give thanks."

The two girls spent the rest of their time chatting about other things. Sal told her about a new male teacher who'd just started at the school, and who had caught her attention.

"It's about time, Sally Anne Wheatley. I was frightened you were going to be old maid." Lizzy's eyes sparkled as she teased her best friend.

"And what's wrong with that? I quite like being single. I can do what I want, when I want. It has its benefits."

Lizzy shrugged and placed her knife and fork together on the plate and leaned back in her chair. "I guess so. I have to admit I enjoyed my day in London. But I don't know I'd enjoy it forever." She took another sip of her squash and then folded her arms. "You know, I thought you and Mathew might have gotten together."

Sal's eyes widened and she let out a laugh. "And you would have been alright with that?"

Lizzy chuckled as she shook her head. "I don't know. It would have been a bit strange."

"Well, it's unlikely to happen." Sal leaned forward. "I didn't want to tell you this before, but Mathew's started seeing someone."

Lizzy jolted upright. "Who?"

"Remember that girl at College who was a bit older?"

"The quiet one who had that funny hair style?"

Sal nodded, her eyes bright. "It's her."

"Really? I wouldn't have thought she was his type."

"Lizzy, no one has been his type since you. I think it took him as long as it took you to get over it."

Lizzy sighed and looked at the young couple who were just leaving. "All I can say is just as well we had that sermon this morning." And with that, they also stood and walked arm in arm to the car.

CHAPTER 13

*T*hat evening, Lizzy called Nessa. *Please let there be some positive news and tell me it's okay to come back.* The weight in her stomach argued against the possibility. Even with Sal's reassurance, what she was doing to Daniel screamed 'blackmail' in her conscience. Nessa would agree with Sal, but it didn't lift the heavy guilt from her heart.

As she picked up the receiver and dialled the number, her fingers shook and she almost rang the wrong number. The phone rang for ages, and Lizzy was just about to hang up when Nessa answered, sounding quite breathless.

"Sorry to have made you run, Ness."

"No problem, Lizzy, we've just come in and I heard the phone. I thought it might have been you. I'm sorry, Liz, but there's no news of Daniel."

Lizzy slumped in the chair. That definitely wasn't what she wanted to hear.

"In fact, Riley couldn't find him when he went out last night to look for him."

Lizzy forced her tears back and tightened her grip on the receiver.

"Do you have any idea where he might be?" Her voice was faint and weak, and a feeling of dread flooded through her.

"Not really. The bar maid at the pub said she hadn't seen him for a couple of days, and Johnno hasn't seen him either, so we're not sure. Riley will go out again tomorrow after work and try to find him."

Lizzy gulped and took a deep breath. This was even worse.

"He has to be okay, Ness. I feel really bad for leaving him the way I did. He must hate me right now." Lizzy sniffed and slumped further in the chair.

"Oh Lizzy, stay strong. He's probably feeling a lot of things right now, but that's a good thing. One day soon he'll wake up and see sense. I'm sure of it.

"I hope you're right, Ness. It's so hard being away. Harder than I thought it'd be." She gulped and took a deep breath. "You know, sometimes I think that being with him the way he is would be better than not being with him at all."

"I can understand how you're feeling, but Liz, you're really only thinking about the short term. Just think what it would be like in all the years to come if nothing changed. Do you think you'd cope, let alone be happy, especially when you have a baby around?"

Nessa had a point. Would she be able to cope living with him year after year if nothing changed? Maybe not. A day or a week possibly, but not years and years.

"So, what should I do if he decides not to get any help? Because that's a possibility, isn't it?"

"Mmm. That's a hard one. But yes, I guess it's possible. If that happened, you'd have to really think seriously about how much you want to be with him."

Lizzy pulled herself up. "But we're married, Ness. I've never considered not going back. But I almost feel like I'm blackmailing him, telling him he needs to get help before I will."

"You really are doing it tough, aren't you, you poor thing? There'll be an answer, Liz, one way or the other. God won't leave you high and dry. But if you did come back and he hadn't got any help, you'd have to agree on very clear boundaries. You'll have to do that anyway, even if he does get help, but it'll be harder if he hasn't. Anyway, you need to give him more time. And no, I don't think it's blackmail. It was a reasonable thing to do, given the circumstances."

Lizzy sniffed and wiped her nose.

"Thanks Ness. You always seem to know what to say."

Nessa gave a half-laugh. "I don't know about that. I just wish I could do more."

When Nessa ended the conversation, Lizzy hugged the receiver to her chest. It was her only form of contact with Daniel, as tenuous as it was, and she wanted to hold that thread as long as she could. *Where was he?* Not knowing was horrible. All she could do was pray that God would be with him, wherever he was, and that He would draw Daniel to Himself.

She looked up when Sal entered the room sometime later.

"Any news?"

Lizzy shook her head, and the tears she'd been holding back started to slide down her cheeks.

"Oh Liz." Sal bent down, and wrapping her arms around Lizzy, comforted her until her tears stopped.

WITH DANIEL so much on Lizzy's mind, sleeping was always going to be a challenge, so she and Sal watched a James Bond movie on television to get her mind off him. The choice was limited, and although not great Bond fans, they agreed it was a better option than 'The Way We Were'.

Curled up on the couch with Sal, munching on popcorn and sipping on hot chocolate, Lizzy tried to concentrate on what was happening. For a while she lost herself in the world of espionage, but every now and then an image or a thought would pop into her head and remind her that Daniel was missing. No, not really missing, just no one knew where he was. *But God knows where he is. Oh God, please be with him.* How was she ever going to sleep?

Once the movie was finished, it was way past bedtime, especially for Sal who had to get up and go to work the following morning. Lizzy climbed into bed and pulled out the Janette Oke novel Sal had given her to read. Maybe it wasn't the best choice to be reading right now, but she was loving Marty's journey, and the way God showed His love to her through all her trials and troubles.

She read into the small hours of the morning, devouring Marty's story, clinging to the hope that if God had blessed Marty like He had, maybe He would also do the same for her. By the time she put the book down, her mind had settled, and she rested in the assurance that God wasn't just watching over her, but over Daniel too.

"LIZ... ARE YOU AWAKE?"

Lizzy stirred and forced her eyes to open, shielding them from the sunlight pouring in through the flimsy lace curtains. Where had the night gone? She pulled herself up and focussed her attention on Sal. How did she always manage to look so fresh?

"I am now. What time is it?"

"Eight o'clock... I've got to go, Liz, or I'll be late." Sal walked over and gave Lizzy a big hug. "I'll be praying for you, kiddo. Come back whenever you want. I'm always here for you, you know that, don't you?"

Lizzy's heart burst with love for her friend. How blessed she was to have Sal in her life.

"Yes, and thank you, Sal. I don't know what I'd do without you."

"Go on. Enough of that nonsense. Lock the door on your way out, will you?"

"Of course."

Sal turned to leave.

"Sal..."

Sal stopped and turned around.

"Thank you. I mean it."

Sal met Lizzy's gaze, and an unspoken understanding passed between them. They would always be there for each other.

CHAPTER 14

*A*s the bus took Lizzy ever closer to her home and her father, she breathed in and tried to hold on to God's strength. Mathew's sermon remained fresh in her mind, as did her resolve to forgive her father. As hard as it was to say she forgave him, to live it out would be harder still. She'd never really considered what she'd forgiven him of. There were so many things. She'd been under his control most of her life, from being on display at riding shows, to him trying to marry her to Terrence. Becoming a teacher instead was her first time she'd stood her ground.

Lost in her thoughts, Lizzy almost missed her stop. Luckily for her, the bus driver stopped and called out, otherwise she would have ended up in town. She climbed down the steps and thanked the driver. Gwyneth was there waiting for her as promised, and got out of the car to greet her. Lizzy had told her not to bother, but Gwyneth had insisted, saying it was too far to walk in her condition.

"How was your weekend, dear?" Gwyneth asked after giving her a warm hug.

"It was good, thank you, Mother. I got a lot of things sorted."

"Including Mathew?" Gwyneth raised her eyebrow and studied her daughter.

"Yes, including Mathew." Lizzy smiled inwardly, glad that at last she was able to think of Mathew without an aching heart. She settled herself into the seat and looked ahead. "We spent several hours together on Saturday." She turned her head to her mother and gulped. "I found out why he broke it off, and he also confirmed it was his mother in that photo."

"That must have been a difficult few hours?"

"Yes, it was. It was upsetting, to be honest, but I'm glad I know." Lizzy paused, tilting her head and taking a deep breath. "It was because of his mother. She took a dislike to me from the moment we met, but I had no idea, she hid it that well. It must have had something to do with her relationship with Father. Mathew didn't know about that either. She just kept telling him I wasn't the one for him, and put so much pressure on him that in the end he had to choose between her and me." Lizzy lowered her head and played with her wedding ring. "He chose her."

"Oh my poor darling. That's so sad," Gwyneth said as she stopped the car just outside the entrance gates. One of the gates had become unhinged and was blocking the driveway. Gwyneth climbed out and moved the gate back.

Lizzy spent the few moments alone to reign in her emotions. No room for self pity or regret any longer.

"Sorry sweetie, I didn't mean to interrupt you," Gwyneth said when she re-entered the car.

"Not a problem, Mother."

Lizzy took a deep breath and fixed her gaze on the rose garden as the car crunched its way up the gravel driveway.

"I was angry with Mathew for not standing up to her, but it's too late for anything to change now, so we just have to get on with our lives." She turned to look at her mother. "Sal told me he's started going out with a girl from college. I'm pleased for him. He seemed so lonely."

Gwyneth smiled at her warmly. "And you've finally let go of him?"

"Yes, I believe I have, at last. Now I just want to get home to Daniel."

"Have you had any news?"

"I called Nessa last night, but no one's seen him for several days. She said Riley would go looking tonight. I'm concerned about him, Mother. I almost wish I hadn't left."

"It must be hard for you dear, but stay strong. I'm sure it will all work out in the end."

"I hope so, Mother. I really do."

Gwyneth parked the car in the garage and they both climbed out.

"Come on, let's go inside. I've got lunch ready."

THE PHONE RANG while Lizzy and her mother were seated at the table having lunch. Gwyneth put her sandwich down and walked to the counter to answer it. Gwyneth's face paled and she gripped the counter tightly.

"Yes, she's here. I'll just put you on."

Lizzy looked at her mother quizzically and mouthed, "Who is it?" Her heart beat rapidly. Something had happened to Daniel. She just knew it.

Gwyneth covered the mouthpiece. "It's the hospital."

Her eyes held deep concern as she passed the receiver to Lizzy.

Lizzy took a deep breath to calm herself before answering. "Hello, Elizabeth O'Connor here."

"Mrs O'Connor," a woman with a clear business like voice responded. "Dr Henderson here, from Hull General Hospital. I'm glad we were able to locate you. Your husband had an accident last night, and he's in Intensive Care. He's in a coma, and has multiple injuries. I don't want to alarm you, but we think you should come as quickly as possible."

Lizzy slumped and her hand flew to her chest. Her heart raced. This couldn't be happening.

"Will he ... will he be alright?"

"We honestly don't know, Mrs O'Connor. He's not in good way. We won't really know until he comes out of the coma. If he comes out at all."

What did she mean? 'If he comes out of it at all...' It couldn't be..... Lizzy fought to gain control of her emotions. It would achieve nothing to break down on the phone to a doctor she didn't know. She took a deep breath and gulped, clinging onto the receiver with both hands.

"I'll come right away, but I may not get there until tonight."

Lizzy straightened herself and held out her hand to her mother.

Gwyneth wrapped her arms around Lizzy, and supported her physically.

"Can you tell me what happened, Dr Henderson?"

"He had a car accident. Ran into a pole from what I hear."

"No one else was hurt?"

"Not that I know of."

Lizzy let out a sigh of relief. She'd had visions of a multi car pile up with bodies strewn everywhere. At least he hadn't hurt anybody else.

"Thank you for telling me, Doctor. I'll organise myself and get there as soon as I can."

Lizzy hung up the phone and collapsed into her mother's arms.

"I'll drive you, Elizabeth. I can't let you go on your own. He's not in a good way?"

Lizzy shook her head and sobbed uncontrollably. She clutched her chest and felt for her cross. *Oh God, I can't lose him now.*

Gwyneth pulled her tighter and stroked her hair.

Lizzy packed in a daze, and before she knew it, she and Gwyneth were on the M5 heading north.

An empty feeling sat in the pit of her stomach the whole way. *What if he dies?* It didn't bear thinking about. She pleaded for God to keep him alive. Had she caused this? Maybe not directly, but indirectly? How could she live with the guilt if he died? *Oh God, you've got to let him be okay. Please.*

The cold darkness that settled over Hull as they entered the outskirts of the city reflected Lizzy's mood. Heavy mist rolled in from the mountains, enshrouding the city in a cold damp blanket. Lizzy shivered as she climbed out of the car in the hospital car park.

She and Gwyneth walked to the main entrance and stopped in front of the directory board. The Intensive Care Unit was on the third floor, and as reception was closed, they took the lift directly there.

Lizzy held onto Gwyneth's arm for support. Not knowing what to expect was the hardest thing. She should have asked the doctor for more details. Standing in front of the Nurse's station, Lizzy clung to Gwyneth and waited until one of the nurses stopped what she was doing and peered over her glasses at them. Her friendly eyes and demeanour provided Lizzy with some encouragement.

"Yes, can I help you?"

"I'm Elizabeth O'Connor. My husband Daniel is here…" Lizzy's voice wobbled and caught in her throat.

"Oh, Mrs O'Connor. We've been expecting you. Take a seat and I'll call a doctor."

Lizzy and Gwyneth took a seat, but all Lizzy wanted to do was to see Daniel.

Lizzy spent an eternity waiting for the doctor. Fear immobilized her, while the tortuously hard seat meant she couldn't sit still. Waiting would kill her. How bad was he? Maybe he hadn't made it. Her heart beat faster and her pulse raced. *No God, please let him be okay.*

Finally a young male doctor appeared, dressed in a white coat and looking like he should still be in school. Lizzy had hoped Doctor Henderson would've been there.

"Mrs O'Connor?"

Lizzy nodded and gulped. The moment of truth had arrived.

"Come this way, please." He led them into a small clinical room with a round table and four plastic chairs. They took a seat and waited for the young doctor, who had introduced himself as Dr Miller, to speak. Lizzy grabbed Gwyneth's hand.

"Your husband has been seriously injured, Mrs O'Connor." Lizzy let out a slow breath. *At least he's alive. Thank you God.*

"He's still in a coma, and he has swelling on his brain. We're hopeful he won't have any significant brain damage, but we'll have a better idea when the swelling goes down. He also has severe bruising on his chest and abdomen, and has several broken ribs. He's lucky to be alive, Mrs O'Connor." Dr Miller looked Lizzy in the eye.

Lizzy grimaced. *Poor Daniel.*

Gwyneth squeezed Lizzy's hand.

"How long will he be in a coma?"

"Impossible to say. It could just be a matter of days, but it could stretch out for weeks, even months."

"Can we see him?" Lizzy leaned on her mother for support.

"You can, but he's not a pretty sight. Just a warning."

"It's okay. I just want to see him." Lizzy looked at Gwyneth. How would she have survived without her mother's strength and support?

She followed Dr Miller along the corridor until they reached the room where Daniel lay. The doctor opened the door and ushered them in. Lizzy gasped at Daniel lying in the bed with tubes of all sorts attached to his body. He didn't look like Daniel at all. His face was bruised and swollen, and a deep gash low on his forehead had been stitched. His right eye was black and his head wrapped in bandages.

Lizzy's heart melted at him lying there, so broken and damaged, and she raced forward and sat beside him, taking his hand gently. As she peered into his face for some sign of life, tears rolled down her cheeks.

"Daniel, I'm so sorry. Please come back to me," she whispered to him as she squeezed his hand, but his lack of response only made her tears fall harder. She took the tissue her mother held out and wiped her eyes. Her mother's hand on her shoulder was comforting, but didn't alleviate her pain.

"Can he hear me, doctor?" Lizzy finally asked when she was able.

The doctor was checking the monitor, and stopped to answer. "Probably not, but best to assume he can. Just speak to him normally. It often helps when comatose patients start to come out of their coma to have someone they know there for them."

"Thank you." Lizzy turned back to Daniel. She'd stay here with him until he woke up. She couldn't live if he didn't. So lost in her grief for Daniel, she'd forgotten her mother was standing behind her until Gwyneth squeezed her shoulder and suggested they get something to eat.

"You need to look after yourself, Elizabeth, for the baby's sake. Come on, let's get some dinner, and then we can come back for a while."

Lizzy almost had to be dragged away, and only agreed to leave when Dr Miller promised to let them know if there was any change.

Gwyneth guided Lizzy out of the room and down to a large cafeteria where she bought sandwiches and cups of tea. Being quite late, there was little choice, but in reality, Lizzy wasn't hungry. Worry over Daniel sat heavy in her stomach, leaving no room for food.

"He's in good hands, dear," Gwyneth said as she unwrapped her egg and lettuce sandwich a few minutes later.

"But he's such a mess. I don't know what I'll do if he doesn't survive."

"I'm sure he'll pull through, dear. They'll do everything they can for him."

"I need to stay with him, Mother." Lizzy leaned back in her seat and looked at Gwyneth.

"I understand, sweetie, but you should sleep tonight, and then come back first thing in the morning. They'll let us know if there's any change."

"I guess you're right, but I feel so bad." Lizzy gulped and wiped her eyes with the back of her hand. "He wouldn't be here if I hadn't left him."

"Oh Elizabeth, don't say things like that. You did what you thought was best at the time, and Daniel made his own choices. You're not responsible for that. You didn't put him in that bed. He did it himself. You have to accept that, because it's the truth."

Lizzy sighed as a wave of guilt washed through her body. She wrapped her hands around her cup of tea. "But I know I didn't help. Maybe if I'd been a better wife we could have worked things out and this wouldn't have happened." She sniffed and glanced at the nurses who had just entered. "I just want the opportunity to make our marriage work, Mother. He needs to pull through. He really does."

Gwyneth reached out and took Lizzy's hand. "I'll pray that he will, dear, and trust that God will work it out for good."

Lizzy nodded and gave her mother a half-smile. How full of surprises she was. Fancy her being so spiritual and encouraging.

RETURNING TO DANIEL'S ROOM, Lizzy hoped for some improvement. Just something little. Anything would do. But nothing had changed. Nothing at all. Daniel lay there, hooked up to those hideous machines, still and lifeless. How could she leave him alone in this cold, clinical room?

"But Elizabeth, you need to get some sleep. We'll come back first thing in the morning."

Gwyneth was insistent. Lizzy finally gave in, but before she left, she squeezed Daniel's hand and gently kissed his cheek.

"I love you Daniel," she whispered as she skimmed her lips over his battered and bruised face. "Please come back to me."

CHAPTER 15

"You'll need to tell me how to find your place, Elizabeth," Gwyneth said as the BMW sprang to life in the hospital car park.

When Lizzy realized her mother had never been to the apartment, her chest tightened. *Had Daniel been staying there?* She'd gathered from Nessa that he probably hadn't been, but then, maybe he'd been there at some stage, and who knows what he might have done. As there was nothing she could do, she gave her mother the directions.

The street lamps shed a fuzzy yellow glow through the heavy fog. Not surprising really that no one was about when they pulled up outside the apartment a short while later. It was surreal, being here with her mother and not with Daniel. Lizzy could only imagine what her mother would think of it. The building lacked any street appeal, in fact, it was ugly, but Lizzy was proud of how she'd decorated and furnished the inside of the apartment, and hoped it would gain her mother's approval.

Not that her mother's approval really mattered. But it would be nice.

Lizzy held her breath as she slowly opened the door and peeked inside before switching on the light. It appeared that everything was as she'd left it, and she slowly exhaled.

"Come on in, Mother. Welcome to our humble abode."

Gwyneth looked around as she undid her coat.

"This is very nice, dear. Small, but homely." Lizzy took her mother's coat and hung it on the hook.

"Thank you, Mother. We were going to start looking for a house, but then all this happened. I guess we'll be stuck here for a while now. If Daniel survives, that is." Lizzy's shoulders slumped and a sudden wave of fear gripped her body, sending a cold shiver up her spine. *What if he didn't survive?* She couldn't imagine what it would be like if he didn't.

"Oh darling." Gwyneth pulled Lizzy close and comforted her. She gently stroked Lizzy's hair and whispered to her. "God's looking after him. Trust Him, dear." She slowly released her hold on Lizzy and held her at arm's length. "Come on now Elizabeth, dry those tears and show me to my room."

Lizzy sniffed, a faint smile growing on her face. "Thank you for being here, Mother."

Gwyneth's eyes watered, and she squeezed Lizzy's hands.

With Gwyneth settled in the spare room, Lizzy ventured into her own bedroom. Her and Daniel's bedroom.

Everything was as she'd left it the morning she'd gone looking for Daniel just over a week before. Her heart ached. *Oh God, please let him pull through.* She fell onto the bed, not even bothering to change, and clutched Daniel's pillow to breathe in his scent.

LIZZY WAS WOKEN by her mother at six o'clock the following morning with a cup of tea.

"Elizabeth! You slept in your clothes!" Gwyneth said as she placed the cup on the bedside table.

Lizzy looked at the crumpled smock she'd had on since leaving Sal's place the previous morning and grimaced.

"I must have fallen asleep without realising." She pulled herself up and reached for the cup of tea. "Thanks for waking me, Mother."

"I thought you'd be anxious to get to the hospital, dear. Although I'm sure you'd also benefit from a sleep in."

"Yes, I am anxious. I wonder how Daniel is this morning?" She put her tea down and slid out of bed.

"I doubt there's been any change," Gwyneth said as she walked back out to the kitchen, followed by Lizzy.

"I want to be there when he opens his eyes." Lizzy stood looking out the window and drank her tea. "I'll finish this and get ready quickly." She glanced at her mother, who was already dressed and ready for the day. "You must have been up early, Mother."

"No earlier than usual, dear."

"Oh... I hope you slept well?"

"I won't complain," Gwyneth replied, taking a seat and picking up a piece of toast.

Lizzy tilted her head to her mother as she washed her cup and placed it upside down on the draining rack. So strong and stoic. Love for her mother warmed Lizzy's heart.

"That sounds like you didn't…"

"Yes, well. Strange bed and all. It's not a problem, dear."

"Okay then. As long as you're okay, I'll leave you to your toast and jump in the shower."

Fifteen minutes later, Lizzy was showered, dressed, and ready to leave for the hospital.

WHEN THEY ARRIVED they went straight to the ICU and stopped at the Nurses' station, where they learned Daniel was still in the same room, and that his condition was unchanged.

Lizzy led the way, and stopping at the door, she took a deep breath to still the shaking in her hands before opening it slowly. The nurse was correct. Daniel lay in the same position, his face empty of expression. Only the bandage on his head looked any different. Everything else about him was just as it had been the night before.

She walked swiftly to the chair beside the bed and took his hand, saying good morning to him before placing a gentle kiss on his cheek. She had to be strong for him, but inside she was a mess. She pushed back the tears that stung the back of her eyes and took a slow, deep breath.

"Well, Daniel O'Connor. What are we doing today?"

When he didn't answer, Lizzy proceeded to tell him about their trip into the hospital that morning in rush hour traffic. It had taken twice as long to get there that morning as it had taken to get home last night.

"And you know what I discovered when we got home? You

haven't been sleeping in our bed!" She leaned closer to him. "Where have you been, Daniel? What have you been doing?" She peered into his face, hoping for some reaction. Just a flinch or a twitch. Just something to let her know he was okay. But there was nothing. Lizzy's heart fell, and she pulled back a little, her body slumping. "Well, you're not going to get rid of me that easily. I'm going to stay here until you wake up, so you'd better make it snappy. I don't want to have the baby while I'm sitting here."

Gwyneth placed her hand gently on Lizzy's shoulder.

"Elizabeth, I think you need some time alone with Daniel. Do you mind if I go off for a while?"

Lizzy looked up startled. How could she have forgotten about her mother? "Where will you go, Mother?"

"Just for a walk. The hospital gardens looked particularly lovely. I'll grab a coffee and find a seat and read for a while. I'll come back later in the morning and check on you."

"Okay Mother. I'm sorry." Lizzy held her hand out to Gwyneth and smiled weakly.

"Nonsense, dear. Daniel needs your attention, not me."

Lizzy let her hand drop and thanked her mother. When Gwyneth had gone, she turned to Daniel, and as she gazed at him and gently stroked his hand, love for him flowed through her body like warm honey.

"Daniel. I don't know if you can hear me or not, but I'm sorry for everything. I know I didn't love you as I should, but that's all sorted now, and I just want you back. I love you, and I promise we'll work everything out together." She leaned in closer to him and kissed him on the cheek. "Just come back to me, please." She closed her eyes and squeezed back the tears that threatened to fall. She had to stay strong, for both their sakes.

As she sat beside him stroking his hand, she told him all about her week, including the meeting with Mathew and how she'd finally been released from his hold on her. She told him about the church service, and how she'd forgiven Mathew and his mother, and that she'd also forgiven her father. It all came off her lips so easily, but would she have been able to talk to him like that if she knew he could hear?

"It's like a clean slate, Daniel. We can start again, without any of those shadows hanging over us. I know we can do it, Daniel. I just know it."

Lizzy sat quietly, and prayed for Daniel and their marriage. She pleaded with God to bring Daniel back to her, whole and undamaged, and that she'd learn to love him more, and to be the wife he needed. One that would support and encourage him, through thick or thin. One that would love with him with God's love, unconditionally.

She studied his face. The bruising and cuts told a story, and not a nice one. *But how will it work if you keep drinking, Daniel? How can I love you unconditionally if you continue to drink and lift your hand to me?* Nessa's words came back to her as she reflected on this seeming disparity. *'Lizzy, you'll need to set boundaries...'* Boundaries...

Nessa! Does she know Daniel's here? Lizzy sat up, her heart pounding. How could she have forgotten about Nessa and Riley, especially after all they'd done?

She stood up and was about to go looking for a phone when a woman doctor walked in. She had a friendly face and short ginger wavy hair, and Lizzy knew instantly this was Doctor Henderson.

"Mrs O'Connor?" The doctor stretched out her hand towards Lizzy's.

Lizzy nodded and took her hand.

"Doctor Henderson. The nurses told me you were here. It's nice to meet you."

"It's nice to meet you too, Doctor." Lizzy shot Daniel a glance. "He doesn't look too good, does he?" Lizzy's voice faltered. "Please tell me he'll be alright."

"We certainly hope so, but it's a matter of waiting. Apart from looking after his physical injuries, we can only wait for him to come out of the coma himself. Hopefully it will only be a matter of days."

The doctor picked up Daniel's chart and inspected it.

"Everything seems fine here. He'd be very sore if he was conscious, so maybe it's best he's unaware of it all for now."

The room started spinning, and Lizzy fumbled for the seat.

"Are you alright, Mrs O'Connor?" Doctor Henderson strode over and helped Lizzy to sit.

Lizzy looked up gratefully and nodded.

"Yes, I think so. It was just such a shock seeing him like this, but hearing it from you ..." She reached out to Daniel and took his hand. "It must have been a bad accident. Do you know what happened?"

Doctor Henderson stood with her arms crossed low in front of her and tilted her head. Her face softened further as she spoke. "Not all the details, but I believe it was a single vehicle accident, and he was intoxicated at the time. I hate to tell you this, dear, but the police will want to interview Daniel when he regains consciousness."

Lizzy closed her eyes. It was as she'd feared. Why had Daniel been driving when he'd been drinking? She could throttle him. He knew better than that, surely. But maybe this was the rock bottom Nessa had referred to. At least he hadn't injured anyone else. She inhaled deeply and opened her eyes.

Squeezing her lips together, Lizzy nodded acknowledgment. The doctor placed her hand gently on Lizzy's shoulder.

"Can I call someone for you?"

Lizzy sniffed and shook her head. "My mother's not far away. But thank you."

"'No problem, dear. It looks like this couldn't have happened at a worse time for you. Make sure you look after yourself."

Lizzy nodded and smiled gratefully at the doctor.

"I will."

When the doctor left, Lizzy remained seated to calm her nerves. Having the Police involved was something she hadn't anticipated, and the very prospect filled her with apprehension. Leaning forward, she clenched her hands together and controlled her breathing, inhaling and exhaling slowly.

She was interrupted by a nurse who had come to check on Daniel, so took the opportunity to visit the bathroom and then to call Nessa.

"Nessa, Lizzy here." Lizzy gripped the receiver with both hands, and leaned against the wall for support.

"Lizzy! We've been trying to contact you. Where are you?"

"I'm at the hospital. We left as soon as we heard and got here late last night. Oh Nessa, it's horrible!"

"I know sweetie. We were there yesterday for a while. He's a mess."

Lizzy sniffed and wiped her nose with a tissue.

"He's in good hands, Liz. He'll pull through."

Lizzy nodded and closed her eyes. "I hope so," she said weakly.

"Stay strong, sweet girl. Is somebody with you?"

"My mother at the moment. But she has to go home today."

"Come and stay with us then. You won't want to be on your own."

Lizzy sniffed and gulped before replying feebly. "Thank you, Ness."

"I'll come to the hospital this afternoon, and we can sort out what to do then."

Lizzy nodded, her heart overflowing with an array of emotions, including a sense of relief to be able to share her grief with Nessa.

"Thanks Nessa," Lizzy whispered before hanging up.

LIZZY PULLED a tissue out her pocket and wiped her eyes, annoyed with herself for not even being able to make a simple phone call without bursting into tears. Why couldn't she be strong like Sal or Nessa?

Once she'd regained control of herself, she returned to Daniel's bedside, where she remained until Gwyneth returned half an hour later.

"How was your walk, Mother?" Gwyneth's cheeks looked

flushed and her normally tidy hair slightly out of place.

"Quite relaxing, dear, although a chilly wind was blowing." She pulled her jacket off and placed it over a chair. "And how are you?"

Lizzy pulled herself straighter, determined to be strong.

"Good. I met Doctor Henderson, and I've spoken to Nessa. And there's been no change with Daniel." She looked at him, longing him to wake him. Nothing, not a single thing, had changed. How much longer would it take?

Gwyneth smiled warmly at Lizzy and held out her hand. "Be patient, dear. It's early days yet."

That word again. Her mother was right. She'd always wanted things to happen straight away, patience not being one of her strong points.

"Nessa said I can stay with them."

"That's a nice offer, dear. Better than being on your own. I feel bad about leaving you, but I promised your father."

"It's okay, Mother. You drove me here." Lizzy stood and gave Gwyneth a warm hug.

"It was the least I could do, dear." Gwyneth leaned back and held Lizzy at arm's length. "I'll be praying for you both, Elizabeth. Despite what your father thinks, I believe Daniel is a fine young man, and I'm sure once he's faced his problems, he'll make you a wonderful husband."

Despite her resolve to be strong, Lizzy couldn't control her tears. Her mother's words warmed her heart and gave her hope for their marriage. Yes, Daniel was a fine young man, and he would make her a wonderful husband. Despite all the odds, they would have a future to look forward to together. *You just need to wake up, Daniel.*

CHAPTER 16

*D*ay after day Lizzy sat beside Daniel's bed, holding his hand, talking to him, reading to him, and praying for him. Day after day there was no change, apart from the fresh dressings the nurses applied. They washed and shaved him, making him comfortable, but the expression on his face remained unchanged.

Lizzy ran her fingers over his body when no one was watching, imagining what it would be like to be in his arms again, to have him love her like he had when they were first married. She remembered their honeymoon and how affectionate he'd been, and she laughed at how many clothes she'd packed but hadn't needed.

She whispered to him and told him how much she loved him, and made promises she hoped she could keep if ever he came back to her.

She read to him from the Bible, praying that the words might filter into his heart, even if his ears were unable to hear.

AND THEN ONE DAY, as Lizzy read aloud from the book of John, his monitor sent out a series of piercing beeps. Startled, she dropped her Bible and stood, her heart beating faster as panic set in. Moments later, two nurses flew in through the door.

Lizzy stood back, her eyes wide and pulse racing, as the nurses checked the monitor and pressed the alert button. Within seconds, two orderlies appeared and transferred Daniel, with all his tubes, to another bed, and wheeled him out with Lizzy following, her arms reaching out to the trolley.

Lizzy frantically tried to get past a short, stocky middle aged nurse who stood in her way, but the nurse held out both arms and prevented her from going any further.

"You can't go with him, dear. He's had a haemorrhage in his brain, and we need to operate straight away. You can stay here or in the waiting room, but you can't go with him."

"Please let me follow him." Lizzy's eyes popped as she pushed harder to get past the nurse.

"WALK WITH ME."

Lizzy walked with the nurse down the hallway until the orderlies pushed the trolley with Daniel lying on it through a pair of swinging doors with a 'No Entry' sign very obviously placed above, and disappeared. The nurse directed her to the waiting area, and then left.

On her own, Lizzy's heart raced out of control and she thought she would faint.

"Are you alright, Mrs O'Connor?"

Lizzy looked up with a pained expression on her face. "I just need my husband to be alright."

"It's too early to tell, I'm sorry, but we'll let you know the moment we have news."

Lizzy inhaled deeply and clenched her hands together. *God, why did you let this happen?*

The nurse placed a cup of hot tea in Lizzy's hands without her noticing. Lizzy stared at the swinging doors, and every time someone came out, her heart lifted, but then fell when they walked past her.

She turned when someone sat beside her. Nessa placed her arm around Lizzy's shoulder and pulled her close. Time inched forward slowly and painfully, one slow second at a time.

WOULD DANIEL SURVIVE? *Oh God, he has to. Please be with him.* Lizzy remained in Nessa's embrace, suspended somewhere between hope and despair. Her mind drifted briefly from time to time, but then she'd be brought back to the horrible reality of the situation as the sound of the doors swinging open reached her conscious mind. How much longer could this go on for?

Finally a doctor she hadn't seen before stood in front of them. Lizzy looked up expectantly, desperate to hear that Daniel had pulled through, but scared to hear he hadn't. The look on the doctor's face didn't tell her anything. Her eyes pleaded with him for an answer.

How long can he just stand there for? Her heart screamed out for an answer, and yet she was unable to speak. Everything happened in slow motion.

Through the thick fog, his voice came to her.

"Mrs O'Connor, your husband is one lucky man. We got it just in time."

It was a dream. Had he really said that Daniel was going to be okay? Why had she doubted? Lizzy slowly came out of her fog and absorbed the wonderful news. Daniel had survived! Tears of joy and relief rolled down her cheeks as she hugged Nessa tightly. Her heart felt like it would break, such was her elation.

ALTHOUGH DANIEL HAD SURVIVED the blood clot, he was still in a coma. Lizzy determined to stay at his bedside, and despite pleadings from Nessa to come home and sleep, she stayed there, night and day, only catching a few hours' sleep here and there in an armchair the nurses brought in for her.

Two weeks after Daniel's accident, Lizzy felt a twitch in his fingers while reading to him. She jerked her head up, wondering if she'd imagined it, much like the first time she'd felt the baby move. She peered into his face as she called out to him, but there was no reaction. Maybe she'd imagined it.

She continued reading, but then it happened again. This time she called a nurse.

It was true. Daniel was starting to regain consciousness, and Lizzy was delirious with joy. Her prayers had been answered! But then, her elation was short lived when the doctor told her it could still take days, possibly even weeks, for him to fully regain control over his body and mind, and they still weren't sure if he'd suffered any lasting brain damage.

But it didn't matter! He was coming back, and she didn't

care how long it took. When the doctor left, she leaned her head gently on his chest, and carefully draped her arm over his body. Her smile stretched from ear to ear and her heart filled with love for him as she caressed his body and listened to his strong heartbeat.

That evening, Daniel opened his eyes, and Lizzy was ready for it. She'd been waiting all afternoon, ever since she'd felt that first movement. But she wasn't prepared for the empty stare she received when she looked into his eyes. Yes, the doctor had warned her not to expect too much too soon, but shouldn't there be at least be some sort of recognition? But there was nothing. Her heart cried out for Daniel to see her. Really see her.

Once again, she'd need to be patient. It seemed God was using Daniel's injuries to work on her own issues.

Daniel's eyes didn't remain open for long, but Lizzy remained alert for any further movements, and was rewarded as he occasionally lifted an arm or twitched a finger. She whispered to him constantly, encouraging him to come back to her. She fell asleep with her head beside him on the bed and her arm draped over his chest.

Sometime during the night, she was woken by a nurse checking on him, and she moved back into her chair. The baby must have been squashed, as it began to kick once she sat up. Lizzy gently rubbed her tummy, and her heart warmed as she thought ahead to the time when the three of them would be a real family together.

Over the next few days, Daniel gradually regained consciousness, and Lizzy was elated. Very slowly, he became aware of her and his surroundings, and with every improvement, Lizzy gained hope that he would make a full recovery. She continued to read to him from the Bible, even though she knew he might tell her to stop at any moment. But she couldn't think of any better book to read. She prayed that God's word would be embedded in his soul, and would breathe new life into his heart and mind.

As she read, God was also speaking to her. Verses 2 and 3 in James 1 pointed directly at her. *'Consider it pure joy, my brothers and sisters, whenever you face trials of many kinds, because you know that the testing of your faith produces perseverance.'*

Maybe God was indeed growing her through the trials she and Daniel were experiencing, but how did He expect her to 'consider it pure joy'? Did it really mean she should be welcoming these trials in order to grow in perseverance and character? But who in their right mind would welcome suffering in their life? She would have preferred to grow without it, if truth be told.

Maybe this was part of the journey she was on, and she should be open to whatever God wanted to teach her. How could she expect God to work in Daniel's life if she wasn't open to Him working in her own?

Two days after he first opened his eyes, Daniel spoke to her. Lizzy wasn't sure at first, but she stopped reading, and waited to hear it again. Daniel slowly reached his hand out, and as she looked down and gently took hold of it, he spoke her name. It was faint, but it didn't matter. Daniel had spoken to her.

She looked into his eyes and knew in that moment he'd be okay. His body was still a mess, but his eyes held a promise that he would be coming back to her. Lizzy couldn't hide her joy. Her face beamed, and warmth radiated through her body.

The next day, he spoke a few more words, and by the end of the week, he was able to put together a sentence. The doctors were confident he didn't have any permanent damage, and once his physical injuries had improved a little more, they'd try to get him up. In the meantime, they would move him to a lower care ward.

Lizzy called her mother and told her the good news. Gwyneth was ecstatic, and said her father would also be pleased.

"Will he really?" Lizzy asked, hoping that somehow this might actually be the case.

"Yes, dear. I had a good talk to him when I returned, and I believe he's now a little more accepting of the situation. I think he's realising he might have judged you both a little too quickly."

Could this really be happening? Could God be at work in her father's life as well? It was too much to hope for but it sure sounded as if He was!

"Mother, that's great news! I'm so pleased to hear that." The grin on her face stretched from ear to ear.

Nessa and Riley were also regular visitors at Daniel's bedside, and encouraged Lizzy to come home for a good sleep. Lizzy agreed to think about it, but she had no choice. The privileges she'd enjoyed in the Intensive Care Ward weren't extended to the lower care ward and she wasn't allowed to stay with him over night.

LIZZY WENT home with Nessa the day Daniel was moved.

"We're so glad Daniel's pulling through, Lizzy," Nessa said as she drove towards her home. "He certainly had us worried for a time."

"Not as glad as I am!" Lizzy sat quietly for a moment before continuing. "I hope this is the rock bottom you mentioned he'd have to hit, Ness. I can't imagine it getting any worse."

"I think so, Liz, but there's still no guarantee he'll stop drinking. You'd think if something like this happened to you, it'd really make you stop and think about what you're doing, and hopefully it will, but it's still totally up to him to make the decision." Nessa shot Lizzy a glance as she turned a corner. "Don't push him, Liz. Be patient. Let him go at his own speed."

Lizzy grimaced. What Nessa was saying was right, but oh so hard.

"That's my problem, Ness. I just want everything to happen straight away. I think God's trying to teach me to be patient."

She took a deep breath and looked at Nessa. "You'll need to talk to me about those boundaries you mentioned, but maybe not now. I'm just happy he's awake and improving every day. He'll probably still be in hospital for weeks anyway."

"Hopefully he'll be out before the baby comes," Nessa said as she pulled up in front of their house.

"That would be good - very good!" Lizzy opened the door and climbed out.

ALTHOUGH SHE WOULD HAVE ENJOYED Nessa and Riley's company, the sight of a proper bed was too much, and as soon as she'd eaten, Lizzy excused herself and went to bed.

The pillow felt so soft, and she snuggled into the blankets, pulling them right up to her neck. Within minutes, she was sound asleep, and didn't stir until the following morning when the sounds of young children jolted her awake.

Lizzy spent some time with Nessa and the children, but couldn't keep her mind off Daniel.

"Ness, I need to go back to the hospital. Do you mind?" Lizzy asked when she could get a word in over the din the children were making.

"Of course not, sweetie. We'll get ready and go."

CHAPTER 17

*W*hen Lizzy arrived at the hospital mid-morning, Daniel was sitting and looking much better. The bandages around his head had been replaced with smaller patches, and the stitches had been removed from the cut on his forehead. He was clean shaven, and his hair had been brushed. But best of all, he was reading the Bible Lizzy had left behind.

He started as she walked in and put it down. Was he embarrassed, or did he just put it down because she'd turned up? She recalled Nessa's words. *'Take it slow. Don't push.'*

Lizzy walked over to him, and bending down, kissed him gently on the lips, allowing them to linger on his just a little longer than they possibly should in public, but she didn't care. Daniel was alive and well, and no one was going to stop her from kissing him.

She pulled up a chair and took his hand. Leaning close, she

traced the outline of his face with the tip of her finger, her eyes not letting go of his.

"You don't know how much I've waited for this day, Daniel O'Connor."

He squeezed her hand and the faintest of smiles grew on his face.

Lizzy rested her head against his chest, and he lifted his hand and stroked her hair. Warmth radiated through Lizzy's body as all the tension of the previous weeks slipped away.

THEY COULD HAVE STAYED like that forever as far as Lizzy was concerned, but eventually she had to sit up. The baby was making itself known, and she was in discomfort.

Daniel was asleep, so she carefully extricated herself from his body and once standing, gave her back a good rub. Was she ready for this baby? Her preparation had certainly been interrupted, but all seemed to be going well, although she was behind in her check-ups. She made a mental note to call the clinic. But what did she know about being a mother? The thought concerned her now the time was coming near. She really knew nothing about caring for a baby, but then, she'd have Daniel to help her, and he should know. She looked down at him and her heart overflowed with gratitude to God for bringing him back to her.

He stirred, and his eyes opened. She took his hand and gently squeezed it.

A SHORT WHILE LATER, once Daniel had eaten the lunch he'd

been given and Lizzy had been to the cafeteria to get a sandwich, the time had come to ask Daniel for his version of what happened. She'd heard from various people that he'd been on the A63 heading west when he veered off the road and hit a pole. But where was he going, and why?

She sat beside him, leaning slightly forward, his hand in hers. Her heart rate had increased slightly, and it took a while for her to speak, being unsure of where it would lead.

"Daniel, do you remember anything at all about the accident?"

His eyes lifted and his body tensed.

"It's okay. I'm not angry, Daniel. I just want to know what happened, and where you were going, that's all." She stroked his hand with her thumb and leaned her arm on the bed beside him.

He looked away and Lizzy's heart fell a little.

"If you don't want to talk about it, it's okay, Daniel." She continued stroking, but pulled back a little. Maybe he wasn't ready just yet, and she'd have to put some of that patience into practice.

Just when it seemed he wasn't going to answer, he cleared his throat. She lifted her head and her gaze caught his. His mouth was downturned and he shook his head.

"I don't know Lizzy. I really don't. It's a blur in my mind." His eyes had that faraway look, as if he was in another place and time. "I remember being at the pub. I'd had a few, and I decided to go and find you." He looked into her eyes. "That's about all I remember."

Lizzy didn't know what to feel. Part of her was elated that he wanted to find her, but then she also carried guilt that she'd indirectly caused his accident. No, she couldn't let herself think like that. She recalled her mother's words - *'it was his choice to drink, not yours'.*

She squeezed his hand and her smile grew warm.

"Thanks, Daniel. At least I know where you were going." She took a deep breath and grimaced. "The Police want to talk to you."

Daniel closed his eyes and hung his head. Lizzy sat still, her heart beating rapidly.

Opening his eyes a few moments later, he lifted his head slowly.

"I've wrecked everything, haven't I?"

She leaned forward and clutched his hand. "No, you haven't, Daniel. Please don't think like that. As long as we're together, we'll be okay. We can work it out, I promise." Her eyes pleaded with him, and her breathing was heavy. She just wanted to hug him and assure him of her love, but his ribs hadn't quite healed.

Tears welled up in his eyes.

"I don't know what I've done to deserve you, Lizzy. You had every right to leave me." The remorse in his eyes was genuine and warmed Lizzy's heart. "But I was so glad to see you here. I didn't ever expect you to come back."

"Oh Daniel. I said I would. It was never in my mind to leave you forever. I just didn't know how to cope with your drinking, not being used to it and all."

"I'm sorry Lizzy. I really am. We're in a mess now because of me." He turned his head to the side and gulped.

"Daniel, look at me." She waited until he looked at her before continuing. "It doesn't matter. It really doesn't matter.

We can sort out the mess. The main thing is that you're okay and we're together."

Daniel held her gaze and then nodded slowly. He held out his arm and she leaned into him gently. Yes, as long as they were together, it would be alright. It might not be easy, but they'd be alright. *Thank you, God.*

DANIEL'S RECOVERY CONTINUED SLOWLY, but each day he grew stronger. He asked Lizzy to read to him, as he couldn't keep his eyes open long enough to read much for himself. She was surprised when he asked her to read from the Bible. "But don't get your hopes up," he said when she raised her eyebrows and smiled excitedly.

"I'm just figuring it didn't work my way, so maybe I should try a different way. But I don't want you preaching to me, right?"

Lizzy nodded her head vigorously.

"Right. I promise."

She chose to read the book of John to him, but had to stop regularly to answer his questions. When she got to the story about Nicodemus, he asked her to read it again, and wanted her interpretation of what it meant to be born again.

This was really putting her on the spot. She'd expected God to somehow just change Daniel, but now he was wanting her to explain things. If she stuffed up, she'd lose her chance. No, she couldn't think like that. God was here with her. She loved Him, and her faith was strong. She'd never doubted Him, ever since she'd committed her life to Him when she was at university.

But her faith had been more private. Apart from praying for people and going to church and reading her Bible, she'd never really shared her faith with anyone. Would she be able to get the right words out so they made sense, or would she make a mess of it and as a result, lose Daniel's interest?

No, she had to trust God to give her the words. After all, she really just had to share what in her heart she knew was true. If she was honest and genuine and sincere, surely God would bless that.

OKAY, here goes... "When Jesus was talking to Nicodemus, he tried to make it easy for him to understand by using an illustration of a newborn baby entering life. What He was saying is that to begin a new life with God, we have to start again. Jesus called it being 'born again', but these days it's also called 'being saved'. We don't literally have to go back to being physical babies, but in a spiritual sense, we do. Being 'born again' or 'being 'saved' is the actual moment we start that new life, but understanding how God made it possible is the first step."

"Alright, I think I've got that. I guess you'd better tell me how, now that we've started." Daniel straightened himself a little and then settled back against his pillows.

Lizzy smiled inwardly. How exciting it was to be sharing about Jesus with Daniel after all this time.

She breathed deeply before continuing.

"The simple answer is just a few verses down, in John 3:16: *'For God so loved the world that he gave his one and only Son, that whoever believes in him shall not perish but have eternal life.'*

"There must be more to it than that. Just believing doesn't sound enough."

"Well, yes and no. I guess it comes back to what *'believes in him'* actually means. It doesn't mean just head knowledge. It means that you really believe in everything about him. How he came, why he came, and why he died. Oh, and also that he rose again. Just a minor point." Lizzy lifted her eyes and realised she may have confused Daniel. Why had she joked at a time like this? She quickly went on to explain.

"Not really. Jesus rising from the dead is the key to it all, because if it's not true, and he didn't, well then, all the other stuff is meaningless."

Daniel tilted his head.

"Why did he die in the first place? I know it has something to do with being saved, but it's never made sense to me."

"Well, basically it's because without his death on the cross, no one could have eternal life. The whole reason for His birth, death, and resurrection was to provide the pathway to heaven for sinful mankind who would never get there on their own. It all goes back to Adam and Eve."

Daniel rolled his eyes.

"Stop it!" She waved a hand at him. "Hear me out!"

"Okay then. This might be interesting, I guess." He crossed his arms and looked at her with a glint in his eye. It was good to see the old Daniel coming back. "Do you really believe in them?"

"Yes I do. There's a lot to take in, Daniel. But it's also really simple. The gospel in a nutshell is that God created man without sin, but Adam and Eve, the first man and woman, stuffed it up by listening to the snake, who was really the devil in disguise. They disobeyed God, and as a result, all of mankind was tarnished with sin and condemned to death, both physically and spiritually.

"But it hurt God so much that his perfect creation was now imperfect, he made a way for mankind to come back to him. And that was to have his perfect Son, Jesus, come to earth as a human, to live a perfect life, and then to become the ultimate sacrifice for all of mankind by dying on the cross. Jesus, who was without sin, chose to take on the sin of the world, my sin, your sin, so that we could be sinless again in God's eyes. Now, when God looks at me, or anyone else who believes in him, he doesn't see our sin. He sees a new creation, pure and clean because of Jesus.

"Oh, and he rose again. He came back from being dead. That proved He was God, and that He just wasn't any old person. Jesus coming back from death shows us that we don't have to worry about dying physically, because Jesus conquered it for us. If we believe in him, we have everlasting life. With God." Lizzy stopped and looked at Daniel. "So, what do you think? Did I do alright?"

Daniel reached out his hand and squeezed Lizzy's, an encouraging grin lighting up his face.

"You did good, Liz. But I'm going to have think about it some more. It kind of makes sense, but it's a lot to believe in. Especially when you can't see God or Jesus."

"Yes, I know. That's where faith comes in, but there's a lot of information you can read that proves Jesus was actually a real person. A lot of people have tried to prove he didn't exist, only to go on not only to believe in him, but to become Christians. And like I said before, it's not just head knowledge. I know deep down in my spirit, or my heart, or whatever you want to call it, that it's true, and that Jesus lives in me. It's just so real. It's hard to explain, but *I know*. I might not be able to touch Him, but He's with me all the time. Anyway, maybe that's enough for today?"

"I think so. I'm feeling a bit tired. But maybe we can read some more tomorrow?"

Lizzy smiled and squeezed his hand. This was way more than she'd ever hoped for, and her heart overflowed with expectation.

"That would be great, Daniel."

THAT NIGHT AT DINNER, Lizzy shared with Nessa and Riley about how Daniel seemed to be softening towards God. Even as she spoke, she had to pinch herself to make sure it was real.

"It's only a start, but it's amazing how open he's become. I can hardly believe it."

"That's wonderful news, Liz. We're so happy for you." Nessa said as she gave Lizzy's hand a squeeze.

"Thank you. I know that even if he does give his heart to the Lord, which I'm really hoping and praying he will, it's still not going to be easy for him, but at least he'll have God in his life and that will make a huge difference."

"Yes, it will. He'll still have a long road ahead of him, but I'm sure once he decides, God will give him the strength he needs."

There was still no guarantee that Daniel would give his heart to the Lord, Lizzy knew that, but there was hope, and she clung onto that with both hands.

CHAPTER 18

$\mathcal{L}$izzy continued to read the Bible to Daniel every day, and every day Daniel had questions for her. She discovered he actually continued reading for himself after she left at night, and often he'd bombard her with questions as soon as she walked in. His hunger to understand was insatiable.

After days of this, the time had come to ask Daniel if he was ready to do something with all this knowledge. Was he ready to accept Jesus for himself? She'd prayed about it the night before, and was confident it was the right time.

Nessa dropped her off at the entrance to the hospital, and she made her way to Daniel's ward. As she turned the corner, her heart fell. A policeman stood at the end of Daniel's bed. She knew it had to happen, but she'd almost forgotten about it.

Lizzy paused, hesitant to interrupt, and turned when a nurse called out to her.

"Mrs O'Connor, you can sit here if you like," the nurse said as she pointed to some chairs not far from the Nurses' station. Lizzy smiled and thanked her, and took a seat.

"How long have they been here?" Lizzy asked as she glanced at Daniel's room.

"About ten minutes I think."

"They didn't want to see me?"

The nurse shrugged her shoulders. "I'm not sure. I'll let them know you're here, just in case."

Lizzy sat demurely with her hands in her lap and her ankles crossed while she waited for the nurse to come back, but inside she was a bundle of nerves. Why did this have to happen today of all days? *God, what's going on? Did I get it wrong?*

The nurse reappeared a few moments later and told Lizzy they didn't need to see her, but they were just leaving, so it was fine for her to go in.

She passed them in the corridor, a burly older man with short bristly hair who walked with a slight limp, and a thinner younger man with dark hair, cut short. Neither looked terribly friendly.

Unsure as to how Daniel would have coped with this meeting, Lizzy paused before she entered his room and took a deep breath. Would he be angry, or would he have just accepted it as an inevitable consequence of his poor choices? She was about to find out...

Daniel sat in bed with his head down and his arms crossed. He looked up briefly as Lizzy entered, but slithered down the bed slightly and lowered his head. Not a good sign.

"Daniel, it's okay," Lizzy said as she leaned over and kissed his cheek. "Whatever happens, it's okay. We'll work through it." She lifted his chin with her finger and kissed him on the lips.

Their eyes connected, but Lizzy's heart fell. The glint had gone and his eyes were now dull.

"No Lizzy. It'll never work." He sighed dejectedly and shook his head slowly. "You won't want to be married to me once I've been hauled before the court."

"Don't make decisions for me, Daniel. You're not the only one who's ever been convicted of driving under the influence, you know. We'll survive this, but we have to be together on it. I'll support you, but don't shut me out, okay?" Her eyes pleaded with him, and she moved closer.

His shoulders sagged further.

"Who knows what they'll give me when they find out about my past. Are you ready for that?" He leaned forward as he spat the question at her.

Lizzy gulped. She'd forgotten Daniel's prior conviction and his time in jail. Maybe it wouldn't come out, given it had happened in Ireland, but it was highly likely it would.

"We'll get through it, Daniel. I promise. Whatever they give you, we'll survive."

Silence hung between them, Lizzy's body rigid as she waited for Daniel's next move.

After several tension filled moments, he lifted his eyes.

"You're persistent, Lizzy, I'll give you that." He paused and pulled himself up. "You know I might get jail time again?"

Lizzy's heart fell. No, she didn't know that. She took a deep breath as she gripped his hand. "I didn't know that Daniel, but I'll stand by you, whatever. I promise."

"Why would you do that, Lizzy? Your father will completely disown you when he finds out."

"Daniel, everyone's responsible for their own actions and

reactions. If Father doesn't agree with my decisions, that's his problem, not mine. But I won't hold it against him. You're my husband, for better or worse, and I'll stand by you, even if he disapproves."

Daniel's face softened to a grin and he squeezed her hand.

"I always knew you had spunk, but now you're proving it." He pulled her close and hugged her gently.

Lizzy rested her head on his chest as he stroked her hair, and tried to force the thought of jail out of her mind.

When she sat up, Lizzy asked Daniel when he was due in court.

"There's no date yet, but it'll be soon after I get out of here."

Lizzy nodded, and fought against the nausea building in her stomach. If Daniel was sent to jail, she'd most likely be without him when the baby was born...

"So Lizzy. How does your God fit into all of this?" His arms were crossed as he once again put her on the spot.

Lizzy took a moment to pull her thoughts together. Why had she ever thought it would be easy? But really, if Daniel was going to make a decision to follow Jesus, it would never work if his commitment was shallow and only made to please her. It had to be real. And he had to see that her own faith and belief was real and could survive the toughest of tests. But would she pass this test? *Oh God, I pray I do.*

She inhaled deeply, and let out a pained chuckle.

"It's like I'm on a quiz show, but the stakes are much higher." The glint in his eye had returned and her body relaxed.

"It's okay Lizzy. Take your time. I'm not going anywhere."

She shook her head at his cheek, but the grin on her face broadened.

"Well, God never promised an easy life with no troubles, even for those who believe in him." The verse she'd read just a few days before came to mind, and she immediately saw God's wisdom in drawing her attention to it at that time. "But He gives us the strength and ability to get through them if we let Him, and as a result, we become better people.

"Giving your heart to Jesus is only the first step. The journey from then on is all about growing more like Him, but we don't have to do it on our own, because He's with us all the way. We just have to be open to Him and allow Him to teach us how to live. It's just like we're little children learning from our parents. It's a life long journey, and sometimes the best way we can learn is by going through tough times.

"So, to answer your question, God will help us through this if we let Him. He's not going to fix it so that it goes away. He doesn't do that. But if we let His Spirit into our lives, and accept the outcome without being angry or bitter, He'll give us His peace and love instead, and will help us handle whatever we have to."

"You really believe this, don't you?" Lizzy looked up into Daniel's eyes and her heart filled with love for him. God was working in his life, she could feel it.

"Yes, I do, Daniel. I can't imagine my life without Him in it. I thank Him every day for saving me and for being with me. I know I let Him down all the time, but He's always there for me."

Daniel remained still and quiet. He was deep in thought, and Lizzy sensed God was touching his heart and reaching out to him.

"Daniel," she said a few moments later. "Do you want to ask Jesus into your heart?"

Lizzy held her breath as Daniel looked deeply into her eyes. Her heart raced. This was the moment she'd been waiting for. *What would his answer be?*

His gaze, steadfast and sincere, held her captive. She couldn't move. *Come on Daniel, please answer...*

He took her hand and patted it gently.

"Yes Lizzy, I do. I want to ask Jesus into my heart."

Lizzy didn't even try to stop the tears trickling down her cheeks. Her heart soared and she hugged him as tightly as she dared.

She slowly pulled back, and wiped her face. "Okay then, Daniel O'Connor. Today you become a child of God - let's do this!"

"What do I have to do?"

"It's simple really. You first have to believe, and I think you do?"

"Yes, thanks to you, I believe."

Lizzy's body tingled. Daniel really believed!

"Then you have to repent." She gulped. *This was going to be a challenge.* "Repentance means that you confess you're a sinner and that you're in need of saving. But it has to be genuine. You have to really mean it, and that's the hardest thing for most people to do, because it makes them face up to their real self."

Lizzy's heart beat rapidly as she waited for Daniel's response. Would he humble himself and confess his sin before God? Or would this be the stumbling block?

"Lizzy, I really am sorry for all the wrong I've done. For the way I've treated you and other people. I can see I've got sin in my life, and I need to get rid of it, so yes, I'm ready to confess."

The remorse revealed in Daniel's words was genuine, and Lizzy thanked God with all her heart.

"Well then, all that's left is to tell God all of that. And then he'll do the rest." She squeezed his hand. "Are you ready?"

His eyes glistened as he returned Lizzy's squeeze.

"Yes."

"Let's pray, then." Lizzy closed her eyes and began.

"Dear God, thank you so much for your love for us. And thank you so much for sending Jesus to earth to die for us so that we can be with you. We don't deserve any of this, but we gratefully accept it. And today, Lord, Daniel wants to accept you as his Lord and Saviour. Please fill him with your love and your peace as he gives his heart to you. Thank you Lord God."

"Daniel, just say this prayer after me, okay?"

Daniel nodded.

"Dear God, I need You to sort me out. I've done some bad things in my life, and I'm truly sorry for them all. Not just things I've done, but things I've thought. I want to turn away from my old life, and instead live for You. Will You come into my life and cleanse me from the inside out? Make me a new person, Jesus. I know I don't deserve You, but I know You love me just as I am, and for that I'll be forever grateful. Thank you Lord Jesus. In your precious name, Amen."

After Daniel had finished praying this prayer, Lizzy stood and gave him the biggest hug she dared. Tears streamed down both their faces, but Daniel was sobbing. Lizzy held him as God washed him clean from the inside out, just as He had done with her many years before, removing the debris and dirt from all the years he'd lived for himself, and replacing it with His love and forgiveness.

A nurse came in while Lizzy was holding him, but Lizzy shook her head and the nurse left quietly. When Daniel's tears finally subsided, he lifted his head and looked into Lizzy's eyes.

"Thank you, my sweet girl. Now I know what you've known all along. That I'm nothing without God in my life. Thank you for showing me that." He pulled her close and kissed the top of her head.

CHAPTER 19

*W*hen Lizzy left the hospital early that evening, Daniel had time to revisit the events of the day. He'd never anticipated he'd feel so different inside, but it was like a weight had been lifted from him, and he felt new and refreshed. Lizzy had shown him 2 Corinthians 5 :17 which explained what he was feeling: *'Therefore, if anyone is in Christ, he is a new creation; the old has gone, the new has come"*, but it was still a little unreal.

He opened his Bible and started reading, but unlike before, it now seemed to make so much more sense. Lizzy suggested he keep reading through the book of John, so that's what he did, and he was blown away by the way Jesus was treated while He was here on earth, and how most people still didn't believe in Him even though He did all those amazing things right in front of their very eyes.

It was like Lizzy said, that unless people want to believe, they won't. Instead, they'll choose to go their own way and do their own thing, even though the God of all creation stood right there in front of them, offering them a whole new way of living. People's stubborn hearts held them back from all they could be in God. Which is exactly what he'd been doing all his life. Until now.

He was still reading when the nurse came to check on him later that evening. Looking up, he smiled at her, and wondered if she'd notice any difference in him. He closed his Bible and placed it on the dresser before holding his arm out.

"You seem chirpy tonight." She glanced at him as she held his wrist. "Must be almost time you left us, I'd say, from the look of you."

It must have been obvious.

LIZZY SHARED the good news with Nessa and Riley that night, and like Lizzy, they were ecstatic. They'd seen the hurt and bitterness he'd been carrying for years eating away at him and showing itself in his unpredictable behaviour.

"We're just so pleased, Lizzy. It's wonderful news," Nessa said, giving her a big hug. "We've prayed for him daily, and now, well, this is great! *Thank you Jesus!*" she said as she lifted her eyes heavenward.

The mood that night was very upbeat. Lizzy called Sal and told her the good news, but something held her back from calling her parents. Her mother would understand, but she wasn't sure about her father.

She found it difficult to sleep, not because she was worried, but because she was overjoyed and her mind was active. It didn't matter. Instead, she prayed and read, and prayed some more, before she finally succumbed to sleep.

THE NURSE WAS RIGHT. When Daniel was visited by the doctor the following morning, he was told he was well enough to go home. The news filled him with relief and concern. Whilst it was great he'd recovered so quickly, it meant leaving the security of the hospital ward, and going back into the real world with all its problems and temptations. But this time he'd have God with him. And he was determined to not let Him down.

When Lizzy arrived, she found him already dressed and packed. The doctor wanted to see her to go through his follow up care with them both, but then they were free to go. As Nessa had already left, they called a taxi and went home.

IT HAD BEEN ALMOST ten weeks since they'd been in the apartment together, since that day Lizzy had made that ultimatum with Daniel. She'd never imagined it would end like this, but she couldn't have been happier. It didn't matter that they didn't have a house. This was their home, and as she'd joked with Daniel on their holiday a few months earlier, she'd be happy living with him in a tent.

After Daniel unlocked the door and they were both inside, he pulled her close and kissed her like she'd been wanting him to for so long. She gave herself to him willingly, and revelled in the closeness she'd feared might never have been theirs again.

CHAPTER 20

The day after arriving home, Daniel received his notice to attend court on Friday of that week.

"They didn't waste any time, did they?" Lizzy said as she stood behind him looking at the piece of paper.

"No, not at all. Are we ready for this?" Daniel faced her and pulled her onto his lap.

Lizzy wrapped her arms around his neck, and leaned against him. "I don't want you to go to jail, Daniel, but we'll survive it if you do. Maybe they'll take one look at me and decide to just give you a fine and a suspension. You never know."

"I'll hate it if I'm not around when the baby comes." He kissed the side of her face, and brushed her hair with the back of his hand.

Lizzy took his hand and placed it on her tummy. "Here, feel for yourself. I think it's in training for a marathon the way it's kicking."

Daniel chuckled and agreed.

The rest of the week was spent catching up on everything, as well as meeting with the solicitor in preparation for Friday's court hearing, and plenty of Bible study and discussion. Daniel wanted to know everything. Lizzy was amazed at his thirst for the Word, and the way he just didn't accept what he read without trying to understand what it meant for him.

DANIEL'S BODY still had some healing to do, so even if he avoided jail time, it was unlikely he'd be able to return to proper work for some time. This knowledge made them take a look at their finances. Their savings had dwindled now that Daniel's pay had stopped and Lizzy had taken leave without pay. Once her maternity leave payment kicked in, they might just survive for a while, but Daniel would need to find a job. They didn't even think about what would happen if he went to jail. And they needed to buy another car. The insurance company refused to pay out as Daniel had been charged with driving under the influence.

"Who's going to give me a job now?" Daniel asked one night as they sat together discussing their situation. "I couldn't find one before, so what's the chance of finding one now?"

His dejected look brought back memories of the old Daniel and sent a shiver down Lizzy's spine.

"You can't think like that anymore, Daniel. We'll pray about it and ask God to open some doors. You never know what He's got in store for you. We just have to trust Him, not only with a job, but also with the court appearance, and with our money. With everything, really. But that doesn't mean we sit back and wait for Him to wave a magic wand and hand us everything already done. You still need to go out looking for a job, but this time, you know that God's on your side. Maybe you'll still get twenty rejections, but you keep going because you know that God has something special for you. And in the meantime, He'll provide for us, somehow, as long as we're trusting Him."

"You sound so confident, Lizzy. I don't know if I can be like that."

"I just know that God won't leave us high and dry. He loves us, Daniel, and He'll look after us."

"I do love you, Lizzy." He pulled her close and kissed her gently.

THURSDAY MORNING, as Daniel was reading aloud from the Bible, Lizzy sat back and rubbed her neck. The change in Daniel had amazed her, and her heart was full of gratitude to God for turning his life around, but she couldn't help wondering how Daniel would cope when he went back into the real world. Would his new found faith be enough to withstand the pressures he'd face?

"Hey you, what are you thinking about?" Daniel closed the Bible and looked at Lizzy with a puzzled expression on his face.

Lizzy looked at him and took a deep breath. They had to talk about it.

"I was just thinking about how wonderful this week has been, Daniel, but I'm a little concerned."

Daniel cocked his head.

"Go on, my love. What are you concerned about? Apart from my court appearance, that is..."

"It's just that we've been protected here, Daniel. Just you, me, and baby Dillon. But there's going to be battles ahead, especially when you go back out to work. Your battle with alcohol isn't over. You'll be challenged by it again and again at some stage, and I really believe you need to get some help before then."

Daniel straightened himself, and drew his eyebrows together.

"No Lizzy. I've got you, and I've got God. And I'm determined not to drink. That's enough. I don't need outside help."

Lizzy cringed inside. Why did he have to be so adamant? But it wouldn't do to force the issue... she'd just have to pray.

She reached out her hand to his, and forced a smile onto her face she didn't feel. A lump sat heavily in the pit of her stomach.

"Okay then. I guess I have to let it go. You know I'm here for you, Daniel, and I'll support you in any way I can."

"Yes, my love. Thank you. I'll be alright, you'll see."

Oh God, I pray that will be the case...

THAT NIGHT, the night before Daniel's court appearance, Riley telephoned and asked to come over as he had something to talk to them about. They agreed, and waited for his arrival.

Daniel let him in, and ushered him to the lounge where Lizzy was resting.

"Don't get up, Lizzy," Riley said as he leaned down and kissed her on the cheek.

"Thanks Riley. Good to see you." She smiled at him as she squeezed his hand.

"Well, I won't keep you long. I've got a proposal to run past you." He cleared his throat and glanced at both Daniel and Lizzy before continuing. "I've heard about a job that might suit you, Danny. A Bible College in the Lakes District is looking for a maintenance person. It's a live-in job, and they're prepared to accommodate a family. The pay isn't great, but you wouldn't have to pay for housing, so it could be a good option. Plus, it's run more like a community, so you get to mix with the students and teachers, and you can sit in on any classes you want. I can put in a good word for you if you like the sound of it."

"Daniel, it sounds perfect!" Lizzy sat up and grabbed his hands.

Daniel laughed and shook his head. "Lizzy, look at you! You're just like a little kid wanting an ice-cream!"

"I'm sorry, I can't help it." She calmed herself a little. "Don't you think it's perfect?"

"Maybe. But we hardly know anything about it." Daniel turned to Riley and tilted his head. "Do you really think it's a job I could do?"

"Easy. It's just mowing lawns, a bit of gardening, keeping things running, all things you've done before. Nessa and I both think it would be the ideal job for you."

"Well, I guess I'll trust you on that. So now it's just a little matter of that court appearance…"

"Yes. That's the sticking point. But we're hoping for a good outcome, Danny. Bill's a legend, and if anyone can get you a lighter punishment, it's him. But you'll have to agree to rehab."

Daniel leaned back and crossed his arms over his chest.

"Why are you so against rehab, Daniel?" Lizzy drew her eyebrows together. "Anytime rehab's mentioned you put up a wall. I don't understand." Memories of their earlier conversation about him getting help came to the fore.

"Do you really want to know?"

She nodded eagerly. "Yes, I do."

Daniel sighed and took a deep drag on his cigarette. "When I was in last time, I went cold turkey. Not just alcohol, I'd been taking some hard gear as well, and it's left a bad taste in my mouth. I don't have fond memories of the place. I don't want to be locked away for weeks on end away from you." He tapped the ash into the tray in front of him and crossed his legs. "I know it works for some people, but just not me. I don't need it, anyway."

Lizzy grimaced and struggled to remain positive. It couldn't all fall apart just because Daniel wouldn't agree to rehab, surely?

"Can't you agree to regular counselling without being admitted? That would surely help?"

Her eyes locked with his as an unspoken battle waged between them.

Riley leaned forward and spoke quietly. "I think you should agree, Daniel. It can't hurt, and might just help. And it might keep you out of jail."

Daniel turned his gaze to Riley. Moments later, he threw his arms up.

"Alright. You both win. I'll agree to counselling."

Lizzy cast her eyes heavenwards and sent up a prayer of

thanks as tears welled up behind her eyelids. She squeezed Daniel's hand and a broad smile grew on her face.

LIZZY COULDN'T GET the news of the possible job for Daniel out of her mind. Although little information had been given, she felt it was from God, and thanked Him for providing for them. Yes, there was a long way to go, but she was confident, and so when it came time to go to court the next morning, she was far less nervous than she might have been, although she'd been battling a persistent headache all night.

That morning, Daniel deliberated over what to wear, but in the end agreed with Lizzy's suggestion of black trousers, white button up shirt and black jacket, although he wasn't happy about it.

"I look like a waiter," he said as he looked at himself in the mirror. "Can't I wear something a bit trendier?"

"No. You look smart and presentable. Just how you need to look in court. I think you look very nice." She reached up and planted a kiss on his lips. "Come on, Riley and Nessa will be here any moment."

She grabbed his hand and pulled him out the door. Riley and Nessa had just pulled up outside the apartment block as they reached the bottom of the stairs. Lizzy held Daniel's hand in the back of the car for the short trip into town. He was fidgety, and she knew he was nervous. There was every possibility he wouldn't be coming home with them.

Nessa must have been nervous too, as she was chatting away in the front about anything and everything. Lizzy did her best to listen and respond when appropriate, but her head hurt, and she just wished Nessa would stop.

The court house car park was almost full, but there were a few spots towards the back. Once parked, Riley turned around in his seat and looked at Daniel. Thankfully Nessa had stopped talking.

"Hey Danny, would you like to pray before we go in?"

Lizzy squeezed Daniel's hand again and tried not to tear up when he agreed.

"Let's pray, then," Riley said as he reached out his hand to Daniel. "Heavenly Father, God of mercy and grace, we know You want the best for Daniel and Lizzy. We don't know what the outcome will be today, but we trust that whatever it may be, You will give Daniel and Lizzy peace and joy. We pray that they will trust You to lead them and be with them in the days ahead. We dare to ask that Daniel might avoid jail time, but we pray that Your will be done. Lord Jesus, I commit Daniel and Lizzy into your hands, and ask that You bless them with your mighty love. In Jesus' precious name, Amen."

The moment passed all too soon, but God was with them, and they knew that whatever happened, they'd be okay. When Riley turned back and opened his door, cold air raced into the car, making Lizzy shiver. She pulled her coat and scarf tighter before she climbed out with Daniel's help.

Hidden between the open doors, Lizzy faced Daniel and gently put her hands on his chest after straightening his collar. "Are you okay, Daniel?" She looked into his eyes and her heart filled with love and respect for him as he looked back at her with strength and determination.

"Yes, I'm more than okay." He brushed her hair with his hand, and held her gaze. "I'm ready for this, Lizzy my love. I'll trust God whatever the outcome, even if it's jail. It won't be forever." Lizzy's heart pounded as he pulled her close and kissed her gently.

"Come on you two," Nessa said with a laugh in her voice. "Anyone would think you'd just got married!"

Lizzy turned her head and gave her a cheeky grin. "Give us a break, Ness. It *is* like we've just got married..."

"I know, I know.... Sorry to break it up, but we do need to go in."

"Okay Ness, settle down. We're coming." Daniel released Lizzy and took her hand as they headed towards to the courthouse.

DESPITE THE FACT they'd only just committed the whole proceedings to the Lord, Lizzy's stomach had an empty feeling, and she gripped Daniel's hand.

Bill McIntosh, Daniel's solicitor, had arranged to meet them at nine thirty in the foyer. Of medium height, he stood erect, giving the appearance of a much taller man. He looked impressive in his dark suit and navy blue tie, and Lizzy prayed he'd be successful in obtaining a lighter sentence for Daniel.

Bill smiled broadly and held out his hand.

"Good morning Daniel, Lizzy." His voice was deep and commanding, and filled Lizzy with confidence. He nodded to Riley and Nessa before turning his attention back to Daniel.

"You're towards the top of the list, so I suggest we wait here." He pointed towards the waiting area where others were already seated.

Daniel and Lizzy took a seat, with Daniel sitting beside Bill. Lizzy was having trouble breathing and didn't feel too well, but hid it from Daniel. She wanted to be so strong for him. As Bill talked to Daniel, she tried to focus on what was being said, but she was feeling light headed and her headache hadn't gone away. *Oh God, please help me get through this, for Daniel's sake.*

She sipped the coffee Nessa handed to her a few minutes later and felt a little better.

Nessa sat beside her.

"Are you okay, Lizzy?"

"Not really, but don't say anything, Ness. I just want to get through this."

"I don't like the look of you. You're all puffed up."

"I'll be okay." Lizzy smiled weakly, and looked up expectantly when Bill said Daniel had been called.

Nessa helped her up and held her arm as they followed behind Bill and Daniel, who were deep in conversation.

Taking her seat in the court room, Lizzy wished she was anywhere but here. Would she be able to focus on what was happening? She really didn't feel too well at all. In fact, she might be sick at any moment.

The magistrate called Daniel to the front. Daniel stood and stated his name, and pleaded guilty to the charge.

She had to get out. Sweat oozed from her forehead, and she felt clammy all over. She attempted to stand, but swayed. Nessa steadied her.

"I need to go to the bathroom," Lizzy whispered to Nessa

while holding her hand over her mouth. As Nessa helped her out, Lizzy's gaze settled on the back of Daniel's head, and her heart ached for him. Why was this happening right now? *God, why?*

"I think we need to get you to hospital, Lizzy," Nessa said once Lizzy had been to the Ladies. "You're very pale, and your face is swollen. I'm really concerned."

"No Ness. I need to be here for Daniel."

"No Liz. Listen to me. You need to look after yourself right now. We're going to the hospital."

Lizzy gave in when she swayed and almost fell. She waited in the foyer while Nessa got the car, and then sat slumped in the front seat while Nessa sped to the hospital.

One look at her, and she was admitted straight away. It was all a blur, as she was prodded and poked by a variety of doctors and nurses. Nessa remained by her side the whole time, holding her hand, assuring her everything would be alright.

"Mrs O'Connor, can you hear me?"

Lizzy tried to focus on the person speaking. She nodded to the vague outline of a male doctor standing over her.

"We need to deliver your baby, Mrs O'Connor."

The words jolted her. *No. This couldn't be happening.* It was too early. She was semi-aware of Nessa beside her, but nothing else made much sense.

She jumped slightly at a prick in her arm, and then she was being pushed through a tunnel. A tunnel with no end. Bright lights flashed overhead, and jumbled sounds of voices and wheels and metal touching metal whirled in her head. Then it all went blank.

CHAPTER 21

*D*aniel held his hands together tightly in front of him to keep them from shaking. As much as he wanted to trust God, he'd still be devastated if he was sent to jail. How could it be otherwise when it'd mean being separated from Lizzy when she was so close to having their baby?

He turned his head slightly at a noise that came from behind. *Lizzy!* He gripped the back of the chair but it was too late. His case had begun.

~

WHEN LIZZY CAME TO, she struggled to remember where she was. A nurse stood above her with a baby in her arms. Lizzy glanced at her stomach, and realized with a start it was her baby. She tried to pull herself up, but winced as searing pain tore through her lower abdomen.

"Don't get up, Mrs O'Connor. Stay right there. May I introduce you to your new little son?"

She must be dreaming. It wasn't real. But no, it was real. She looked down at the tiny bundle that had just been placed beside her. This was unbelievable. She had a son. But how had it happened? And where was Daniel?

She glanced around, but he wasn't there. Her heart fell when the fog in her brain cleared and she remembered he was in court. Slowly it all came back. The trip to the hospital, the lights, the noise, and being told her baby had to be delivered.

LIZZY'S HEART swelled with love for her tiny son. He was perfect, and the mop of black hair was so Daniel. She gently touched his little pink face and kissed the top of his head as she held him in her arms.

She glanced up as Nessa walked in, smiling from ear to ear.

"Lizzy! Congratulations!" Lizzy smiled tearfully when Nessa leaned down and kissed her on the cheek before gazing at the tiny bundle lying beside her. "He's beautiful, Liz." Nessa's eyes sparkled and held tears of her own.

"Thank you, Nessa." She shook her head and looked up. "I don't believe it's happened." Lizzy's eyes widened and she grabbed Nessa's arm. "What happened to Daniel?"

Nessa shrugged and had a painful look on her face.

"I don't know yet, Liz. I haven't been able to find out. I left a message at the courthouse to tell Riley where we were, but I haven't heard anything yet."

"Oh Ness, I'm so worried about him."

Nessa leaned down and hugged her as Lizzy began to sob. "Try not to worry, sweetie. We'll know soon enough."

Lizzy sniffed and tried to calm herself. Every time she moved, it hurt. It was almost too much to take in.

"Here, let me take this little one," the nurse said, leaning down and gently picking up Lizzy's baby. "I'll bring him back shortly once you've had a little more recovery time, Mrs O'Connor. It mightn't hurt to get some sleep if you can." The nurse was right. Maybe it was the after effects of the anaesthetic, but whatever it was, she was very drowsy.

"I think I'll have a little sleep, Ness, but wake me the moment you hear anything from Daniel. Promise?"

"I promise." Nessa smiled at her and squeezed her hand before leaving the room.

"LIZZY, ARE YOU AWAKE?" Lizzy blinked at the sound. "Lizzy, I've got a surprise for you."

Lizzy opened her eyes wide as she recalled where she was. Nessa was standing over her. Was there news of Daniel?

"Here, let me help you up." Lizzy leaned on Nessa's arm and wriggled herself up until she was sitting. Her eyes questioned Nessa, but her gaze averted round her as she caught a glimpse of blue helium balloons being held by someone standing in the doorway.

Lizzy's skin tingled and her grin broadened when she realised it was Daniel.

"Daniel! Oh my goodness! You're here! I can't believe it!"

Daniel raced towards her and hugged her gently as she sobbed in joy. "My precious Lizzy. Thank God you're alright."

He kissed the side of her cheek before pulling slowly away. "And I believe we have a son…"

"Yes Daniel. We have a son. And he looks just like you!"

"Poor little baby! Fancy looking like his daddy!"

"It was a compliment!"

"I know, I was only joking, sweet girl. When can I get to meet him?"

"We can call the nurse. But Daniel," she grabbed his hand and peered into his face. "Tell me - what happened in court? You're here, so I'm guessing you didn't get jail?"

"Yes, thank God. Bill was brilliant. I got off with a fine and a suspension. No jail." Daniel's smile was infectious, and tears welled up behind Lizzy's eyes as all the built up tension fell away.

"Daniel, that's wonderful. I'm sorry I wasn't there."

"Go on with you. You had other business to attend to… So, where is he?" He turned as the nurse entered the room with a tiny bundle in her arms. She leaned down for him to see, and then placed the tiny bundle in Daniel's arms. Lizzy's heart filled with love for the two men in her life as Daniel gazed in wonderment at their son, and she revelled in God's goodness.

Daniel sat gently on the side of the bed with his son in his arms. "What are we going to call him?" He glanced at Lizzy as he allowed the tiny baby to wrap his fist around his finger.

"How about 'Dillon', after your brother?" Lizzy suggested.

Daniel's face expanded into a wide grin. "That's perfect, Lizzy. A perfect name for a perfect boy!" He leaned down and kissed his little son. "Welcome, baby Dillon."

Lizzy leaned over and looked at the baby.

"I think it's my turn," she said with a mischievous grin on her face.

LIZZY SPENT the days following the early arrival of baby Dillon getting to know him, and learning how to care for him. Daniel was brilliant. He had it down pat when it came to changing Dillon, and showed Lizzy a trick or two. Every time she saw him with the baby, she smiled.

She telephoned her mother and told her the exciting news, and she also telephoned Sal. Both were ecstatic. Sal said she'd try to get up to see her, and Gwyneth also promised a visit as soon as she could.

Meanwhile, Riley helped Daniel apply for the job he'd mentioned, and organised for his counselling sessions to start. Daniel told Lizzy he was really looking forward to finally kicking his old habits, even though he wasn't looking forward to the sessions. He said he felt bad that they didn't have a car, but even if they did, he wouldn't be able to drive for another year.

"But I guess it's my fault. I can't blame anyone else."

"We'll be alright, Daniel. We'll sort it somehow."

NOT LONG AFTER she'd been allowed to go home with baby Dillon, her parents told her they would pay a visit the following weekend.

Daniel, although nervous about meeting Lizzy's father again, was determined to prove to him that he was worthy of being Lizzy's husband, and that he was fully prepared to take responsibility for her and Dillon. It just would have been better if he had a job. He'd been waiting to hear whether his application had been successful, and had been checking the mail box every day. The interview had been the week before, and he'd been told he should hear within the week. The interview had gone well, and he was surprised at how keen he was to get the job.

Yes, it would mean living in a community environment, and yes, he may feel a little threatened, but it didn't matter. It'd be an opportunity to learn and grow, and to mix with Christians who could provide support as he learned to live his new life with God and without alcohol. He'd told Lizzy all about it, and they'd prayed about it, and although they agreed they'd trust God for the outcome, he was still on tenterhooks about it.

The Friday before Lizzy's parents came, Daniel picked up the mail and it was there. He carried the envelope to the kitchen where Lizzy was making tea, and stood before her with the envelope in his hand.

"This is it, Lizzy love."

"Well, go on. Open it." She stopped and studied him. "You're nervous, aren't you?"

Daniel nodded as he stared at the envelope.

"You're not going to find out if you don't open it. Do you want me to do it?"

He held her gaze and breathed deeply.

"No, I'll do it." His heart pounded in his chest as he carefully opened the envelope and took out the piece of paper.

Lizzy bent her head so she could see, but he turned it away from her. "Let me look first."

Lizzy didn't need to see it, however, as a moment later, Daniel's whole face exploded into a huge, beaming grin.

"I got it! I got it!!" He wrapped his arms around her and planted a kiss on her cheek as they jigged up and down together.

"Daniel, that's wonderful news! Congratulations!"

~

THE FOLLOWING DAY when Roger and Gwyneth arrived, Lizzy's heart expanded with pride when Daniel was eager to tell them his good news. Her father also appeared to be making an attempt to be friendly, and was less officious looking than normal. Maybe holding his tiny grandson for the first time softened him a little. Whatever the reason, there was hope that Daniel and Father might at last be able to remain in each other's company without an argument.

As ROGER and Gwyneth prepared to leave, Gwyneth caught her husband's eyes and tilted her head as if she was trying to tell him something. Lizzy caught sight of this and wondered what was going on.

Roger coughed and cleared his voice.

"Elizabeth," he paused and glanced at Gwyneth before turning to look at Daniel. "And Daniel... we have a gift for you."

Lizzy raised her eyebrows and glanced at her mother,

puzzled. They'd already given them a huge basket full of baby clothes and baby items. What more could there be?

"Best come downstairs," Roger said, pointing to the doorway with his outstretched arm.

"I'll wait here with little Dillon," Gwyneth said, walking over to look at the sleeping baby.

"Are you sure, Mother?" Lizzy asked.

"Yes, off you go." Gwyneth shooed them out the door.

"What's all this about, Father?" Lizzy asked as they walked down the stairs together with Daniel following.

"Just be patient, dear. You'll see in just a few moments."

He led them to where his car was parked, but surprised Lizzy by continuing past it before stopping at a red Ford Fiesta hatchback.

Lizzy looked at him, and then back at the car, her mouth and eyes gaping as he handed her the keys.

"Go on. It's yours."

Lizzy couldn't stop the stream of tears that began to flow as she threw her arms around her father.

"Thank you, Father! I don't believe it," she said as she bent down and inspected the car. Stepping back, she reached out for Daniel, and put her arm around his waist. This could go well, or it could cause an argument between him and her father. The old Daniel would never have accepted a gift like this from him, but what would the new Daniel do?

She looked at her father and then turned her head to look at Daniel as tension filled the air. Their eyes locked together. Daniel was fighting a battle, there was no doubt about it. Everything within her pleaded with him to accept the gift graciously. Her heart stopped while time stood still.

She breathed out slowly when he broke the silence.

"Roger, you needn't have done this."

"I know, Daniel. But we wanted to. Please accept it as a gift for you both. A peace offering?"

Roger held out his hand towards Daniel.

Lizzy held her breath again and then let it out as Daniel slowly reached out and shook Roger's hand.

"Well, go on then. Take a look." Roger walked over to the car and unlocked it for them. Lizzy hesitated before climbing in, and relaxed when Daniel chose the passenger side. She inhaled the new car smell before inserting the key into the ignition and starting it. It was so quiet compared to the old Escort. Turning her head, she smiled broadly at Daniel. How much more could they take?

When they walked the stairs back up to the apartment, Lizzy hugged her mother and planted a kiss on her cheek.

"Thank you so much Mother. It's beautiful!"

"Our pleasure, Elizabeth. Consider it a wedding gift."

Lizzy chuckled and caught her mother's eye. It was so good to be on better terms with her parents after all this time.

"Thank you so much for coming all this way," Lizzy said to her parents as they made their way to the door. As a last minute thought, she asked, "You wouldn't consider staying would you?"

Roger and Gwyneth both stopped and looked at each other before turning back to Lizzy.

"It would be alright," she assured them when they hesitated. "The bed's made up, and we'd fit somehow. I can't promise a good night's sleep, however." She grinned as she glanced at little Dillon lying peacefully in Daniel's arms.

Gwyneth smiled warmly and squeezed Lizzy's arm.

"That would be lovely, dear. Roger?" She tilted her head towards him and raised her eyebrows.

"I don't think I could say no. She'd never forgive me." He shrugged with resignation and then grinned at Lizzy.

"So I take that as a yes?" Lizzy glanced from one parent to the other.

"Yes, dear, we'd love to stay," Gwyneth said, before giving Lizzy a hug.

LIZZY WAS AMAZED at how well behaved her father and Daniel were that night. What a difference a few months had made. No longer were terse words spoken, in fact, they were deep in conversation for a good part of the evening. Her mother had been working on him, and at last he'd seen sense. Lizzy wondered if the time would ever come when she could quiz him about his relationship with Hilary Carter, or maybe that would be going too far. Time would tell.

DANIEL WAS due to start his new job in two weeks, just before Christmas. In that time, he and Lizzy packed up their apartment, and arranged for their belongings to be moved to the small cottage that was to be their home. Riley and Nessa helped as much as they were able, and Riley told Daniel his counselling sessions would be transferred to one of the staff members at the college.

Moving day finally came, and Lizzy was as excited as a small child about to go to the spring fair for the first time at the prospect of moving into a proper house, after she'd feared so recently it would never happen.

Although Daniel had described the cottage to her, she was in no way prepared for her reaction when it first came into sight.

"Daniel, it's simply perfect! I couldn't have wished for a lovelier place!" Lizzy jumped out of the car and ran with her arms wide open towards the white picket fence surrounding the small thatched roofed cottage. Window boxes overflowed with bright yellow pansies and dark blue lobelia, and all sorts of other pretty flowers that somehow managed to bloom despite the chill of the season. She reached the fence and turned around, stretching her arms behind her and threw her head back, allowing her long unruly hair to fly freely in the breeze, and her heart soared.

"You like it, then?" Daniel looked at her with a cheeky grin on his face.

"Like it? I love it!" She turned around and opened the gate, before remembering one little thing. Dillon. *Dillon! How could I forget him?*

Lizzy spun on her heels and began to head back to the car, when Daniel caught her in his arms.

"He can wait. This can't." Daniel wrapped his arms around her and gazed into her eyes. With one hand he brushed the hair from her face. "Lizzy, what a happy man am I. A beautiful wife, a handsome son, a cottage of our own, a job to die for, and new life in Jesus. What more could a man ask for?"

Lizzy's heart swelled with gratitude to God for blessing a marriage that seemed doomed for failure not that very long ago, and for taking her and Daniel, and little baby Dillon, by the hand and bringing them to this place where they could grow closer to each other and to God.

She held his gaze and looked into his eyes. Yes, they still held mischief and a glint, but they also now held purpose and resolution. Life with Daniel O'Connor would never be boring, but he was a changed man, and she longed to make a start.

"Kiss me, Daniel." Her eyes drew him in, and his hold on her tightened before he lowered his mouth over hers.

~

Daniel and Lizzy's story continues in Book 3: "Beyond the Shadows"
Read the first chapter now!

BEYOND THE SHADOWS - BONUS CHAPTER

"THE SHADOWS SERIES BOOK 3"

CHAPTER 1

*L*akes District UK February 1982

D<small>ANIEL</small> <small>THREW</small> the telephone receiver back into its cradle and thumped the wall.

How dare Da return! Twenty years gone, and he waltzes on in, and expects everyone to come running. The hide of the man! Inhaling slowly, he shook his head and fought the anger swelling up inside him. *Not on your life, Da. Not on your life. Even if you're dying.*

Clenching his fists, he stared out the window at the mountains in the distance without seeing them. Just when everything was falling into place. He'd been doing so well. Three months sober. Hadn't even felt like a drink. But now... no, he must stay strong, for Lizzy's sake. He ran his hands through his hair. *God, give me strength. I can't handle this.*

Life had never been so good - he and Lizzy loved living at the College. Why should Caleb expect him to drop everything and come running back to Belfast to see the man he hated most in this world? How did Caleb even get the number?

So many memories. So much pain and hurt. He'd pushed their ugliness away for so long. Why should he be forced to revisit the past? He had a new life. A life full of happiness and peace. Going back was the last thing he wanted to do.

Daniel looked up and clenched his muscles. *That's it. I won't go. Nobody can make me. Not Caleb. Not Da. Not anyone.*

~

"Look Dillon, Daddy's home."

Lizzy held their three month old baby to the window as Daniel drove the tractor towards the shed and excitedly pointed out his daddy. Her heart skipped a beat as she caught sight of Daniel's strong, masculine frame atop the tractor. Wearing his heavy sheepskin jacket and colourful beanie, even from a distance he caused her heart to flutter.

Although almost two months had passed since Daniel began his job as a groundsman at the College in the Lakes District, Lizzy was still in awe of the way God had provided for them. She adored the little cottage where she and Daniel lived. Yes, it was small and basic, but compared to the apartment in Hull, it was paradise. She'd already planned what flowers and vegetables she'd plant when spring came, but until then, she'd busy herself making the cottage into a home.

As much as she loved being a mother and a homemaker, Lizzy missed her friends and her job as a teacher. With Daniel gone early each morning, and the weather too cold to venture outside with baby Dillon, her days were long. Daniel's homecoming was the highlight of each day.

Daniel had surprised her with his devotion to his job and to the Lord. Since giving his heart to the Lord several months earlier while recovering in hospital from his car accident, he'd been hungry for the word and so keen to learn how to live as a Christian. Every day he asked God to give him strength to withstand the hold of alcohol on his life, and every day he gave thanks for one more day of sobriety. He'd also recently made the decision to give up smoking. Lizzy had suggested he wait. It wasn't a problem for her, and besides, staying sober was way more important. But Daniel believed he should. He'd been convicted about how badly he'd abused his body over the years before coming to Christ and was committed to making amends.

Daniel's new found vigour for life warmed Lizzy's heart. The memories of the old Daniel had faded, and rarely, if ever, did she worry about how he'd treat her when he came home from work or whether he'd been drinking. Instead, she yearned for his company more than ever.

He'd taken the responsibility of being the head of his family very seriously, too seriously, Lizzy sometimes thought. Whenever she broached the topic of her going back to work when Dillon was a little older, Daniel stated emphatically there was no need. It was his job to look after her and Dillon. For now, she willingly complied. No use putting undue pressure on their relationship. It was like he needed to prove he could do it.

Lizzy accepted that for now, this was her life. Spring would soon arrive, allowing her to venture out more often. At least they'd gone to town to celebrate their first anniversary just a few days ago. Although Lizzy looked forward to it, leaving Dillon for the first time made Lizzy anxious. She had no qualms about Robyn's ability. After all, being the Principal's wife, and a grandmother of three, Robyn's experience spoke for itself, but Dillon was so tiny, and so dependent. Lizzy knew he'd be fine for the few hours they were out, but it felt strange not to have him with her.

They enjoyed a lovely meal at the Gardens Restaurant in Ambleside, the nearest town to the College. The restaurant adjoined the Lions Head hotel, and Lizzy breathed a sigh of relief when Daniel only briefly glanced at it on their way in. Every time he passed a hotel he was tested, and so far he'd passed with flying colours.

TONIGHT AS DANIEL walked in the door, something was wrong. Normally he'd be happy and his eyes would light up as he reached out for Dillon, but tonight, trouble sat on his face, and Lizzy's heart fell.

She pulled Dillon tighter and followed Daniel to the bedroom. He hadn't even kissed her. Standing in the doorway, she watched with dismay as he pulled off his work clothes and put on a pair of jeans and his favourite rugby jumper without even showering.

She sat beside him on the bed as he pulled on his boots. "Daniel, what's the matter? Talk to me."

"I need to go out, Lizzy. Please don't try to stop me."

LIZZY FOUGHT HER ALARM. It wouldn't pay to over react. This was the exact situation they'd planned for, but hoped would never happen. Before they left Hull, Nessa and Liam explained what could happen as Daniel weaned himself off alcohol, and helped them formulate an action plan. Lizzy found it challenging to step back and allow Daniel to take responsibility for his decisions, and to trust he'd make good ones, especially after all they'd been through. It would've been so much easier for her to take control, but Nessa advised against that.

"You have to give him room, Lizzy. But don't make it easy for him to drink. If he asks you to drive him to town for that purpose, you have to refuse, unless you feel physically threatened. That's a whole different ball game. He's made the commitment to stay sober, but if he does drink, it's not the end of the world. You just go back to square one and start again. Hopefully he'll be strong, and that won't happen."

But it was happening. Why else would he go out on his own? Lizzy breathed in slowly. Her heart pounded in her chest. She held onto Dillon, cradling him into her shoulder. She had to stay strong for his sake.

"Do you want to talk about it?" Lizzy placed her hand gently on Daniel's leg. If only he'd share the reason for this sudden change in behaviour.

Daniel finished tying his laces then stood, pulling Lizzy into his arms.

"I'm sorry Liz. I need to be on my own for a while. It's not you. It's me. I need some space."

It took all her strength not to cry as she gazed into his troubled eyes. If only she had the right words to stop him. Her hands trembled and a sick feeling grew in the pit of her stomach. Somehow she had to retain control of herself. Nessa had said not to plead with Daniel, or to over react. *Easier said than done.*

"Okay. I won't stop you, Daniel, but please don't do anything you'll regret. Just remember, God's with you, and you can draw on His strength to help you get through whatever it is that's troubling you."

"I know that Lizzy. And I'll try." Daniel's normally confident voice strained with emotion. He pulled back from her and sighed dejectedly. "I guess you won't drive me to town?"

Lizzy's shoulders slumped. It was tempting. Maybe he'd change his mind on the way, and he'd come back home with her. But she had to carry out the plan. That's what they'd agreed.

"No, Daniel, I won't drive you. I'm sorry."

"Okay then. I'll walk."

Lizzy bit her lip and blinked back her tears. *God, please give me strength.*

How easy it'd be to give in. She could agree to pick him up at a set time. But that wasn't what they'd agreed. She wasn't to do anything that made it easier for him to drink. Besides, walking might give him time to sort out the problem. *Whatever it was.* But why couldn't he share it with her? Memories of Daniel's deception when he lost his job flashed through her mind. He'd promised never to hide anything from her again. And he'd been such a different person since giving his heart to the Lord. The old Daniel had reappeared, and she didn't like it.

"I'll pray for you." She reached out her hand and gently touched his cheek, her eyes searching deep within his. His eyes flickered. Was he weakening? But then he spun on his heels and headed out the door.

Every bone in her body wanted to follow him, but she remained strong, and instead of racing after him, she cradled Dillon and pleaded to God to keep Daniel safe.

LIZZY'S HANDS shook as she tended to Dillon. Once he'd settled, she picked up the phone and called Paul. As head of the College, Paul provided the counselling to Daniel that was a condition of his rehabilitation program agreed to by the court. Calling him was part of their plan.

"Paul, it's Lizzy here." She gulped as she tightened her grip on the receiver. "I hope you don't mind me calling, but something's happened, and Daniel's walking to town." She bit her lip and forced herself to stay calm.

"I had a feeling that might happen. He got a phone call at lunch time and was in a dark mood all afternoon. Didn't want to talk about it."

Lizzy's mind raced. *A phone call?*

"Did he say who it was from?"

"No, he didn't say a thing. Didn't even finish his lunch."

"That's strange. I have no idea who would have called him. I'm trying to think."

"I tried to talk to him several times during the afternoon, but he just retreated into himself. It's the first time I've seen him like that. I was surprised, because he's normally been quite open."

"So, what do we do, Paul? I'm really concerned about him."

Lizzy held the receiver tightly with both hands. She had to stay calm, but it was so hard.

Paul sighed heavily on the other end of the phone. "Well, first we pray. There's obviously a battle going on inside him. We knew he'd be tested at some stage. We'll leave him alone for a while, and trust he'll work it out for himself. I'll go to town and look for him in a couple of hours. By that stage he might be prepared to talk."

"Thank you, Paul. I don't know what I'd do without you." Lizzy bit her lip, forcing herself to hold it together.

"It's all I can do, Lizzy. We're in this together. Daniel has a good heart, and he loves God. He's just got to learn to trust Him, as we all do. Let me know if he comes home, otherwise I'll leave about eight o'clock. In the meantime, Robyn and I will pray for him, and I encourage you to pray too."

"I will. Believe me, I will."

$\sim$

To continue reading "Beyond the Shadows", go to www.julietteduncan.com/beyond-the-shadows

NOTE FROM THE AUTHOR

I hope you enjoyed Lizzy and Daniel's journey in **Facing the Shadows**. Their story continues in **Book 3** of the series, **Beyond the Shadows**.

If you haven't done so already, why not join my mailing list to ensure you won't miss any future releases? It's easy to join, and I promise I won't spam you! Just visit **www.julietteduncan.com/subsribe** to join, and as a thank you for signing up, you'll also receive a **free short story**.

Lastly, could I also ask a favor of you? Reviews help people decide whether to buy a book or not, so could you spare a moment and leave a short review? It doesn't need to be long - just a sentence or two about what you thought of the book would be great, and very much appreciated.

Best regards,
Juliette

ALSO BY JULIETTE DUNCAN

The Shadows Series www.julietteduncan.com/the-shadows-series/

"Beyond the Shadows", Book Three in The Shadows Series. Lizzy and Daniel have settled nicely into their new life in the Lake District. Daniel is growing in his Christian faith and Lizzy couldn't be more delighted. Life is wonderful for the young couple until Daniel receives devastating news that may lead to his undoing and challenge his sobriety. With temptation testing him, Daniel will have to draw on God's strength and his family's support to resist it or live with the fact that he's not only failed himself but failed God. Lizzy and Daniel are put to the test. Can they withstand the physical, emotional and spiritual challenges they'll face as they return to Ireland and face Daniel's past? Is their love and their faith strong enough to pull them through or will the pressure tear them apart?

Praise for "Beyond the Shadows"

"This story, for me, was more emotional and really touched down deep in my heart. It was a beautiful story of God's grace, His redemption, His forgiveness and the freedom that is found in all of that. Beautifully written." *Heather*

The True Love Series

After her long-term relationship falls apart, Tessa Scott is left questioning God's plan for her life, and she's feeling vulnerable and unsure of how to move forward.

Ben Williams is struggling to keep the pieces of his life together after his wife of fourteen years walks out on him and their teenage son. Tessa's housemate inadvertently sets up a meeting between the two of them, triggering a chain of events neither expected. Be prepared for a roller-coaster ride of emotions as Tessa, Ben and Jayden do life together and learn to trust God to meet their every need.

PRAISE FOR "THE TRUE LOVE SERIES"

"These books are so good you won't be able to stop reading them. The characters in the books are very special people who will feel like they are part of your family." Debbie J

The Precious Love Series Book 1 - Forever Cherished

"Forever Cherished" is a stand-alone novel, but follows on from "The True Love Series" books. Now Tessa is living in the country, she wants to share her and Ben's blessings with others, but when a sad, lonely woman comes to stay, Tessa starts to think she's bitten off more than she can chew, and has to rely on her faith at every turn. Leah Maloney is carrying a truck-load of disappointments and has almost given up on life. Her older sister arranges for her to spend time at 'Misty Morn', but Leah is suspicious of her sister's motives.

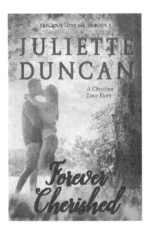

Praise for "Forever Cherished"

"Another amazing story of God's love and the amazing ways he works in our lives." Ruth H

"This book had everything. It was warm and delightful. How it captured my heart and affirmed that God can do anything for all of us if we only believe." Treach

Hank and Sarah - A Love Story, *the Prequel to "The Madeleine Richards Series" is a FREE thank you gift for joining my mailing list. You'll also be the first to hear about my next books and get exclusive sneak previews. Get your free copy at www.julietteduncan.com/subscribe*

The Madeleine Richards Series Although the 3 book series is intended mainly for pre-teen/Middle Grade girls, it's been read and enjoyed by people of all ages. Here's what one 72 year old had to say about it: *I am 72 years of age and thoroughly enjoyed this book. I am looking forward to Book 2 with excitement. Your book can be enjoyed by all ages 11-100. It brings back wonderful memories for the young at heart. Thank you for sharing this book with me. Patricia Walters*

ABOUT THE AUTHOR

Juliette Duncan is a Christian fiction author, passionate about writing stories that will touch her readers' hearts and make a difference in their lives. Although a trained school teacher, Juliette spent many years working alongside her husband in their own business, but is now relishing the opportunity to follow her passion for writing stories she herself would love to read. Based in Brisbane, Australia, Juliette and her husband have five adult children, seven grandchildren, and an elderly long haired dachshund.Apart from writing, Juliette loves exploring the great world we live in, and has travelled extensively, both within Australia and overseas. She also enjoys social dancing and eating out.

Connect with Juliette:

Email: juliette@julietteduncan.com

Website: www.julietteduncan.com

Facebook: www.facebook.com/JulietteDuncanAuthor

Twitter: https://twitter.com/Juliette_Duncan

Made in the USA
Middletown, DE
16 June 2021